DAY SWORN

DAY SWORN

DRAGON OF SHADOW AND AIR BOOK EIGHT

JESS MOUNTIFIELD

DISRUPTIVE IMAGINATION

THE DAY SWORN TEAM

Thanks to our JIT Team:

Dorothy Lloyd
Dave Hicks
Diane L. Smith
Jeff Goode
Deb Mader

If We've missed anyone, please let us know!

Editor
SkyHunter Editing Team

LMBPN Publishing
PMB 196, 2540 South Maryland Pkwy
Las Vegas, NV 89109

Version 1.00 September 2021
eBook ISBN: 978-1-68500-446-0
Print ISBN: 978-1-68500-447-7

Dedication:

To those who have lived through seasons where they have to keep getting back up. Again. And again. You're not alone. You're not wasting your energy. I see you.

CHAPTER ONE

Taking a deep breath, I stepped forward. It was time.

My second bonding ceremony.

This ceremony felt very different from the first we'd performed. For one, we had nothing to prove this time. And two, the surrounding audience included more of our friends. Minsheng, Daisy, Erlan, Newton, and most of the folks staying at the warehouse were here, and I knew I had their support.

I glanced at Minsheng to see his proud, beaming face. It made my heart feel lighter as I focused on the three mythicals standing on four points of a pentagon with me. Zephyr was opposite me, Sen next to me, and Roth in between, all of them smiling but focused.

It was almost time, and we'd been practicing this moment for several weeks, enjoying the distraction it had given us and the time alone.

We waited for Sierrathen. Like last time, she had been the council member who wanted to be there to test our bond and show its strength to the Sanctuary and everyone else we'd invited.

I reached out with my mind, ready to take control of the air, earth, and water nearby. I sent comforting thoughts through my bond, especially to Roth, who had never been in this situation before.

It was easy to worry about this, but we only needed to make some stones glow and then show off a bit. I was good with all of that these days.

Sierrathen stepped forward. There was an expectant hush, and she almost seemed to relish the moment. I wasn't sure what else might happen, but it would start with a speech.

"Welcome, mythicals of the Sanctuary and friends. You have come today to bear witness to a sight none of us are likely to see again in our lifetimes. Aella, bonded with Zephyr and Sen, has taken another step toward her future as Henera. They have all bonded with the water pegasus Roth. They are going to demonstrate that bond."

I blinked, surprised by how short the speech had been and grateful it hadn't lasted too long. I always got more nervous while I was waiting to perform. We had to show our bond in action, however, and all at the same time. It had taken us a long time to decide how to show what we were capable of, but Minsheng had helped us.

As soon as Sierrathen stepped back, another member of the council gave us a strange smooth rock each. She placed Roth's on the ground behind him since he didn't have any hands. I placed mine down as well, then we all turned so we could see the rock in front of us but not each other.

I was never sure how this part of the ceremony worked, but each time we'd seen it or been part of it, the rocks had lit up strangely, and I could only hope they would again.

I picked mine up again, feeling the others do the same. The bond between us made me aware of their positions.

There was a silence in the cavern, no one daring to breathe too loudly. Then my stone lit up in a swirl of colors before it settled on a deep brown. I lifted it high in the air.

The crowd roared their approval, and I turned to see all the others with glowing stones as well. Sen stood atop hers, Zephyr held his in one claw, and Roth had his almost-translucent hoof resting on a stone.

They were all the same color, glowing and bright. we let everyone cheer as I mentally asked my three mythicals if they were ready. Sen's grin grew wider, Zephyr dipped his head, and I felt excitement and anticipation from Roth.

A moment later, Sen ran to Roth and bounded onto his back, helped by my abilities. At the same time, Zephyr and I launched into the air. While Zephyr and Roth flew, I pushed air down and away from me, jetting myself upward until I could reach Zephyr. I landed on his back, and he flew around the large cavern.

Zephyr had grown since the last time we had performed a bonding ceremony. He was now full-sized, and the cavern was more crowded than the last time. We flew in a couple of tight circles, then I took control of the rock area we'd been standing on and lifted it to meet Zephyr as he landed. Roth continued to fly.

Once we were back on solid ground, I started lowering

the rock. Before I put it down, I connected my mind to the rock in the ceiling and tunneled a hole through to the surface, reaching for a small stream that ran down the mountain. I completed the tunnel while forming a bowl at my feet.

Water cascaded into the bowl as I widened it, creating a large pool. I controlled the water to ensure it went nowhere else, not a splash on anyone. At the same time, I dampened the sound to make it a silent but stunning waterfall.

At my mental signal, Roth flew at the waterfall from behind. Sen dropped off his back while he was still several feet in the air. I caught her with air, placing her down gently before Roth landed in the middle of the pool.

I still contained the sound, but I let the water arc out and splash a little. The light from the many mirrors in the cavern glinted off Roth, who looked like a standing pool of water.

There were gasps of delight, but most stayed silent, watching and captivated.

To end the show, I stopped the water flow again, redirecting it on the surface of the mountain to its previous path. I didn't close the hole, however, but widened it to let the light through and shine on the surface of the pool. It lit up Roth, Sen, and Zephyr.

Finally, I moved the mirrors that adorned the room to highlight my bonded mythicals. Roth was glistening like water in the moonlight, Zephyr's scales shone a brilliant bronze, and Sen's delicate mushroom shape came alive in new ways.

There were gasps of awe at how beautiful I made the three creatures look.

Come and stand with us, Zephyr said. *You should be in the spotlight with us.*

I considered refusing since I wanted it to be about the amazingness of mythicals and how far we'd come. It wasn't about me and proving anything.

Before I could say no, however, all three of them looked at me, making it clear they agreed. Nervous of the spotlight in a whole new way, I almost lost control of the elements. Taking a deep breath, I lifted myself into the air as gently as I could and floated over to land in the pool between the three mythicals.

The elves watching us cheered louder. I could barely see them with us lit up so much. They appeared darker.

Hoping I didn't screw it up, I began putting the mirrors and lights back the way they had been. I exhaled with relief when it was almost done and the cavern was lit more evenly again.

As I fiddled with the last of the mirrors, not sure where it had been angled before, I noticed Orthelo coming toward us. He reached out with his mind and helped me put it back, and Gwaelon came over to the edge of the pool.

I was about to apologize and ask where they wanted the water to go when he nodded at it and moved to Orthelo's side.

"I think the pool is an improvement. We should make it a permanent feature," he said, smiling at me.

My cheeks flushed as I walked out, taking control of the

water that had wet my clothes and draining it back into the pool so I was dry again.

Sen bounded onto my shoulder, and Zephyr came closer until I could reach up and rest a hand on his shoulder. It made me feel calmer. Minsheng appeared from the shadows.

"That was impressive," he said. "I knew you'd been working on your fine control outside of battle situations, but you keep showing you can do better no matter how good you get."

Again I blushed, not used to praise. In truth, I was only as good as I was thanks to people like Minsheng, who gave up a lot of time to teach me.

Before I could thank him for his part in everything, there was a commotion from the cavern's entrance. The show was over so the elves and other mythicals were leaving that way, but it was clear that someone was trying to get through and calling for the council.

Concerned that something had happened and aware there were elves looking for me, I moved toward the sound of trouble without hesitation. Sierrathen was also heading that way.

One of the centaurs who watched the border came forward.

"Two elves have arrived," he said, briefly bowing to Sierrathen and me.

"New elves?" Sierrathen asked, her raised eyebrows showing her confusion. Mythicals arrived at the Sanctuary all the time, although less often since things had been more peaceful between the human population and mythicals. The Sanctuary wasn't needed as much.

"They're from the...Amcika." The centaur spat the last word.

I gasped. They were the cult of elves who had almost killed me while trying to open a portal to the elven homeworld.

"What do they want?" I asked. "Do they know Zephyr and I are here?"

"No," the centaur replied. "They've requested sanctuary. They say Aella's words to Cherisse and the fight we all put up opened their eyes."

Sierrathen gaped like I wanted to and looked at the centaur, then me. I shrugged, out of my depth. I hadn't expected this. Everyone in that mountain had given the impression they were committed to their cause.

"Bring them before the council, but don't let them see more than necessary," Sierrathen said, her usual authority kicking in.

The centaur bowed once more and hurried off, the cavern empty enough that he could move freely. As soon as he was gone, Sierrathen turned to me.

"We would appreciate your input on this subject. You know more about these elves than anyone here."

"I don't know a lot, but I'll help if I can," I replied, dread gripping my stomach.

I had only been back for a couple of weeks, and I was still struggling to sleep at night and relax after three days stuck in a mountain against my will, cut off from Zephyr and sometimes Sen.

The only good thing that had come out of it had been finding Roth. Now, however, I needed to pull myself together and work out what this was all about.

I knew my way to the council chambers, and I gathered Roth, Sen, and Zephyr, although I considered sending the pegasus somewhere safer. I did not want these elves to know I had another mythical with me. I suspected they wouldn't be leaving again in a hurry.

When we'd been fighting human agents, the Sanctuary had held any who had crossed their borders as prisoners. I was pretty sure it would be the same for the elves, no matter what they had to say for themselves.

The councilors were all assembled, and they had made space for me to sit on one end. Zephyr, Sen, and Roth sat beside me and behind me. The centaur and several other Sanctuary mythicals appeared with the elves.

I only had a second to marvel at how things had changed from me being at loggerheads with the Sanctuary council and having to explain myself to them. Now I was sitting at their table.

I recognized them. One was the earth elemental who had frequently guarded my cell, and the other was an air elemental I had blasted out of the sky a few times in the final battle. They looked impressed as they surveyed the room. Then they noticed my presence.

Their mouths fell open as they saw me with Zephyr towering behind me, Sen perched on the arm of my chair, and Roth beside me. Then they took in the rest of the council.

"Are you the Sanctuary?" the air elemental asked, her voice shaking.

"We're the council for the Sanctuary," Vestan replied. He was the second of the elves on the council panel. He sat in the middle, with Sierrathen on one side of him.

The Amcika elves looked at each other, more than words passing between them.

I exhaled, feeling tense. This wasn't what they'd expected, but what *had* they expected?

"Why have you come to us?" Vestan asked.

"We'd like to request to stay here. Somewhere Cherisse can't get to us."

"Cherisse is the elf in charge of Amcika. Am I correct?" Sierrathen asked.

She glanced my way, and I nodded before either elf could reply.

"Why would she want to get to you?"

"Because elves aren't allowed to leave the mountain and not come back," the earth elemental answered, his eyes widening in surprise at the question.

That confirmed my suspicions. Cherisse, and possibly other elves before her, were running the place like a cult. It didn't bode well for the determination of the rest of the elves about coming after me again.

For the next hour, I listened as the council grilled the two elves on what they knew about Cherisse and the mountain, as well as how they felt about the portals and the world outside the mountain and the cult they'd been born into.

I tried not to judge them harshly, but it was clear they had been told strange things and they didn't realize it was not how the world worked. That said, they appeared to genuinely want to be outside of the mountain and away from Cherisse.

"We'll need to consider your request, but know that

you're safe and will be provided for regardless of what we conclude," Sierrathen said when the council was done.

The centaur and other guards stepped forward again, motioning for the two elves to go with them. I sighed, feeling more than relief when they were gone from the cavern. Despite that, it didn't feel like anything was over. It felt like the beginning.

CHAPTER TWO

It took another five hours to go over everything I knew and what had happened with the Sanctuary and go back and forth as they tried to decide what to do with the elves seeking protection.

Although I felt sorry for the elves, I could understand the council's reluctance to trust them. It gave me insight into the concerns they must have felt each time I'd stood before them and asked for help. Admittedly, they'd been ruder to me than they were to the Amcika elves, but I'd pushed harder for help and answers.

A few times during our discussions, I had gotten the impression I wasn't entirely welcome in the conversation. However, the decision they were making could impact more than the Sanctuary, and someone had to speak up for humanity as well.

"What do you think of them and their honesty?" Vestan asked me outright.

"I think they're scared," I replied, choosing my words

carefully. "Cherisse is powerful and driven. They've either taken a great risk by leaving or Cherisse has sent them here, and I'm not sure which."

"Our course of action is a difficult one if you cannot be sure." Vestan sighed as he spoke, sounding weary.

I blinked in surprise, not sure what to say.

"I think they speak the truth," Zephyr said, weighing in. "They didn't expect to find us here and only asked for safety. Give them that—safety. A place they can learn about the world and make up their own minds about what's right. Be kind to them and show them another way with your actions, and when the time is right, let them leave if they wish to. You cannot do worse than be the better example and show trust. If they take that information right back to Amcika, you will be no more vulnerable than you are now."

My heart swelled with pride at the wisdom in his suggestion. No one had asked him what he thought, yet he'd cut through all the discussions with a mature and simple suggestion.

Zephyr leaned closer to me again and I sighed, realizing how tired I was but also how much I wanted to get back to the training we'd been doing. Especially since I knew that Cherisse and her elves were still very much a threat.

I had been training with marked elements, seeking out areas of the Sanctuary where the masters often trained and other locations where elves other than me had been. It wasn't easy. I still didn't understand how the elves in the mountain had made it so hard for me to wrestle control from them.

The council made their decision, and there were only a few details on how they were going to go about Zephyr's suggestions left to work out. I made my way to one of the large areas the elves and other mythicals ate in and found Minsheng and Daisy there, eating. They looked sympathetically at me and I smiled to let them know I was okay, then sat down on the opposite side of the table.

The elves brought over a bowl of stew for me and appropriate food for Roth, Sen, and Zephyr. Grateful, I ate quickly and asked for more.

The first few times I'd eaten in the Sanctuary, the elves had been surprised by the quantity, but they weren't anymore, so there was another bowlful waiting for me. I'd expected the other elves here to eat a lot too, but few of them pushed themselves as hard as I did. I drained my abilities during training almost every single day.

Here the elves were mostly safe and could train in a more leisurely way that allowed them to focus on many uses for the elements. I loved it in a lot of ways. They'd made me far more skilled. But it also had occasional frustrations.

I needed to be challenged by other elves. There weren't that many strong enough to challenge me, except for the four elemental masters. That's where I planned to head next.

As soon as everyone had eaten, Sen had drunk deeply, and Roth had spent time in water to replenish himself, we made our way to the main area to find the masters.

It wasn't hard, thankfully. An afternoon training session was well underway. I hung back and watched, aware my arrival tended to make waves and interrupt everything for a while.

Erlan was closest, with Seth and several others training to use fire. I found it fascinating how they could make the smallest amount of flammable material ignite. It was the only element I couldn't control yet, although I had tried on several occasions. I had a feeling I was going to need it.

Despite my desire to remain unnoticed by the students for a while, one of the water elementals happened to look our way. That drew the gaze of other students until the usual hush fell over the training grounds.

I tried to smile at everyone watching us before I made my way to the nearest master. Aquilan, the air master, smiled, always pleased to see me. He ushered me over to one side of the main group.

"Well done," he said. "It's good to see you growing so much and becoming one amazing force."

I beamed at him and leaned in for a hug. It was a relief to see someone who welcomed me without having massive expectations.

"Now, tell me what troubles you, my dear," he said as he pulled back.

"I think I am going to need to train to defend us once more, and I'm not sure I can do it alone."

"That's what we're here for. Come. I have heard about some of the things you learned recently, but perhaps if the other masters and I hear more we can work out what we might be able to do about it."

I exhaled, relieved. Aquilan called the other three masters over to him. I spent the next half-hour talking to them about what I knew, emphasizing the marked feel of the elements, then I expressed my biggest concern. How did I fight elves who could steal control and hold onto it far better than I could?

This last problem set the masters to thinking hard. Each had me steal control of a nearby element from them so they could feel it, with the exception of Orthelo, who used fire. He called Erlan over, who was only too happy to oblige in my place.

When all four had been on the receiving end of having their control snatched away and worked out how to return the favor, there was a pause.

"I think there's something we're missing," Aquilan said. "Some knowledge about how the control works. If they're leaving the elements marked by their presence, they're not being gentle enough."

I frowned as I opened my mouth to point out that I had left elements marked as well. Before I could, the masters realized their students were all waiting for further instructions, having finished their assigned tasks.

"Can everyone gather around, please?" Orthelo called before I could react. Zephyr, Sen, and Roth were sitting in the shade nearby while we talked.

The elves all came closer, staying in groups that matched their element while becoming one enormous mass of mythicals. I smiled at those I recognized and tried to catch the eyes of those I didn't to be friendly.

"We'd like to try something entirely new if you'd all be willing. It's going to feel uncomfortable, and we need to be careful. Aella has brought us fresh insight into how our abilities might work, and with it comes a threat to our way of life," Orthelo continued.

The elves looked around, some glancing my way. I kept the smile on my face and didn't show the nerves that made my stomach tighten.

It wasn't easy, but as Ruehnar explained how to take control of elements from another, the focus shifted to him.

While he was doing so, I reached around me with my mind, feeling the state of the elements and how marked they were. There was a faint signature to some of them, but nothing as strong as it had been in the mountain. I could reach out a long way, occasionally finding a pocket of air or earth where one student was in control.

When Ruehnar finished speaking, there was a clamor, some elves panicking and some of them unsure of how to practice. It was also clear that the masters weren't entirely sure how to train the elves in this way.

Get them all to fight you, Zephyr suggested. *Get them all to take control from you. You can practice holding on while they work out what's different about taking control.*

It was an excellent suggestion, and I voiced it out loud, crediting Zephyr for it.

They met this with interested expressions, but I noticed it wasn't universal. I almost backed down and told them all not to worry, but we needed to learn this. The elves Cherisse had in that mountain would not wait around for us to figure it out, especially if they wanted a portal open.

With the masters taking over again, they encouraged me to stand in the middle of the square, each group spreading out to give me space. One by one, I grabbed the elements I could reach and then waited, feeling everything around me. It was rare that I took control and then just felt the elements as they were without trying to change them or manipulate them in any way.

Bialan joined me a moment later, the fire master taking the role with the one element where I could not. He also started several fires, although he did so in containers designed to hold the tricky element.

I took a deep breath, feeling waves of calm emanating from Roth, Sen, and Zephyr as they picked up on my nerves. Sending gratitude back, I gave the masters a nod.

They had the students begin. At first, it took them a while to work out what to do and how, but it wasn't long before I was feeling my control challenged. Although some of the elves could do little more than push at my grip, a few managed to tear some away.

I tried not to be too harsh as I stole them back, using the experience I had fighting elves in this way. There were too many of them to be sure who was attacking my control most effectively, but I could see the shock on their faces when I took it back swiftly and pushed their minds out of my way.

Despite my attempts to be gentle, they recoiled as if it hurt. I almost stopped my attempts right then and there. Many grew braver, however, willing to attack again and push me harder.

As time passed, they pressed, the elves learning fast. I pushed myself harder and focused, learning to respond faster and more effectively.

However, there were too many of them pulling control from my mind in too many different ways for me to fight them all off and reclaim it fast enough.

The elements under my control dwindled until I was

holding only the bubble of air around me, my head aching from the constant barrage. The fire master and his students had stopped, many of them exhausted, but I held on. The elves around me began to tire as well, and several retreated from the fight.

I pushed out again as Zephyr, Sen, and Roth cheered me on. More and more gave up, drained and unwilling to challenge me further.

Slowly the masters stepped forward as my reach expanded again. I considered yielding then and there but I held my ground, waiting for one of them or all three to attempt to challenge me, although it hadn't been what I'd expected when this training session had begun.

Orthelo was first, the earth under my feet almost entirely under his influence before I slipped back into control, trying to be gentle. His eyes went wide, and he took a step back. The others saw his reaction and hesitated, but he nodded at them and encouraged them to continue.

After the fight I'd put up I was more than tired, but I wanted to know how strong I was compared to the elves in the Sanctuary. Some of them had come to rescue me from Cherisse's cult, but few had been students, and the masters hadn't been fighting for control in the same way when we'd been fighting to escape.

Aquilan was next, whipping the air away from me and making me gasp for breath at the speed and fierceness of the attack. I pushed back, closing my eyes to focus on the way his grip was different from mine, caressing it before I found a weakness. I matched the shape he used, finding it easier to take control back.

When I opened my eyes, the air master bowed to me

and tried again. This time I managed to resist his attack better, changing the way I controlled the elements to something vastly different to him to make it harder. It seemed to work since his next attempt felt as if it bounced off.

Before I could firm up my grip and think more about it, however, Ruehnar decided he was done waiting.

For the next few minutes, I struggled back and forth with all three masters, sometimes giving way and at other times regaining control. They didn't go easy on me, growing braver with each attempt. I didn't restrain my abilities, but finally I was beaten, and everything faded. My bond with Zephyr, Sen, and Roth came close to being drained along with it.

Not wanting to lose the bond with my mythicals, I stopped trying and bowed toward all the elves who had tested me. The masters all sagged, panting almost as much as I was.

As if all three were of the same mind, they applauded me. It rippled outward until every elf nearby was clapping. They smiled too, no animosity for how I might have hurt them while I defended myself.

I blinked, stunned. I'd not held up against all of them, but it was clear I'd impressed them nonetheless.

Feeling Zephyr come closer to me, I leaned toward him.

Well done, his deep voice said gently. *I was worried about how we'd defend ourselves if we faced overwhelming numbers, but you grow stronger.*

I didn't beat them all. And these elves had never tried this before.

You still did far more than you were previously capable of.

I smiled up at the large dragon, grateful for his faith in me. When I looked at the masters, the four of them had come closer.

"Thank you, Henera," Aquilan said, his eyes shining with a proud light. "It was an honor to learn from you."

CHAPTER THREE

As I finished training for the third day in a row, I almost passed out, the strain on my abilities more than I could handle. The elves and I had spent time learning how our control worked and how it could be traded, taken, and shared between multiple people.

It wasn't easy, and more than once, I'd come close to breaking my bonds, but I knew it was important that we learn what we could. The masters agreed.

Walking to the elves in charge, I leaned into Zephyr. It was hard on my bonded mythicals to see me practice like this all day and not have as much to do themselves. They *were* learning to work together, and I could often hear them talking and planning ways to help on their own. Roth was taking flying lessons from Zephyr, but it was still dividing us more than I liked.

"You're improving swiftly," Aquilan said. "I wouldn't be surprised if you could fight off every elf in the Sanctuary now."

"No," I replied. I was touched by his compliment, but it

was not true. There were the council members if nothing else. "All the students here grow stronger under your guidance. And—"

"I think we all know it is you doing the teaching these days, Aella," Orthelo interrupted me, his voice gentle.

"There is still plenty for me to learn. I don't know many things you do."

"And that is the way it will hopefully always be. No one lives long enough to learn everything. But you clearly have things to teach us as well." Ruehnar placed a hand on my shoulder. "Now get some rest and take care of yourself. We'll do what we can and trust ourselves."

I nodded, grateful for their kindness but unable to shake the worried feeling I had in the base of my stomach. We were improving, and the Sanctuary elves were more prepared for battle with other elves, but they were underestimating what Cherisse and her cult were capable of.

Heading back to the center of the Sanctuary with my mythicals, I found myself wondering if the two elves who had defected had told the council anything of use about Cherisse's plans. No one had mentioned anything to me. Not that I'd given them much of a chance. I'd been busy.

We need a break, I told Zephyr and the others. *For the four of us to get away and have some fun.*

Once we've eaten and rested, Zephyr replied.

I could feel excitement and pleasure at the idea coming off Roth. Once again, I marveled at how swiftly he'd settled into the group. He had a charm about him that made me smile. Sen had taken to him, often preferring to sit on his back, or wrap her little arms around his neck, holding on tight to his mane while they flew.

It was wonderful wandering along with them now, knowing we were one unit and working together to protect all mythicals. Zephyr swung his head lower to nuzzle into me, no doubt picking up on my thoughts. I could have frozen time and simply spent every moment like this.

We didn't get another step forward, however, before Minsheng appeared, out of breath as he ran toward the training grounds.

"What's wrong?" I asked, the tense feeling in my stomach coming back.

"The President has called for you again. Wants you in Texas."

I blinked, not used to being summoned by one of the most powerful people on the planet, but aware it was an honor.

"We're going to need to eat on the way," I said a moment later. Zephyr and the others were also hungry, and I was low on power.

"He said you didn't have to rush, but he would appreciate you being there before nightfall."

I frowned at Minsheng. It wasn't a short distance between the Sanctuary and the only place in Texas he could want me. It would take us several hours at our fastest speed, and that was with us all helping to fly.

"We'd best eat then," I said and hurried toward the kitchens.

"Daisy is packing you an away bag," Minsheng added as he fell in beside me, his expression serious.

I almost made him tell me what he knew, but I had a feeling he wasn't likely to say what was bothering him if he hadn't already. I had spent little time with him in the last few weeks, and I felt guilty about that. After all, he was my Shishou, my original trainer, but we'd barely trained under him since we returned.

Before I knew what was happening, I'd opened my mouth and begun pouring out my fears and worries while he listened. Getting food on autopilot, I told him everything I'd been holding back and trying to get my head around.

By the time I had finished, Minsheng was looking at me with a strange light in his eyes, almost smiling.

"What?" I asked, not sure I was entirely comfortable being looked at that way.

"You've come a very long way, Aella," he replied. "And you've learned so much. Trust yourself. And trust Zephyr, Sen, and Roth. The four of you are capable of more than you know. In the meantime, I'll see what I can find out. And talk to the organization. They're still very invested in you and...I am too."

I reached out as Minsheng finished speaking, placing my hand on his.

"You're still the person I trust most. I'm only here because of you and how you never gave up on me or counted the cost when the agency hunted us down. Are you going to be okay?" I asked. "Do you want to come with us?"

Minsheng opened his mouth as if to decline my invitation, but then he nodded.

"Is that possible? Seeing one of these portals might give me some useful information on what they do exactly and how we might better defend them from being opened."

"Then I will carry you," Zephyr said as he lowered his head again. "It would be an honor."

Minsheng's eyes went wide. I realized we'd never offered to fly any of our friends around. Zephyr had always either flown solo or with those who needed rescuing. It was entirely possible since Roth could carry me as well as Zephyr could, and we could fly farther and faster than ever before.

It was quickly settled. Minsheng ran off to pack an away bag while I ate as much as I could stomach and made sure Zephyr and the others had everything they needed before we set out.

Daisy reappeared with Minsheng, handing me a familiar bag and grinning at me.

"One day, I want a ride as well," Daisy said. "But I'll join Holfin in learning how these elves make that famous stew of theirs."

I smiled and nodded, hoping she didn't mind too much that we would be leaving her behind.

"It's okay. I've got Erlan here, and Emily has come to stay for a while. Something about her mother being busy elsewhere, acting as a liaison between some elves and humans near the Canadian border."

Lifting an eyebrow, I almost demanded Daisy explain, but I had places to be. I couldn't involve myself in every affair of the mythicals in the country. Sometimes I had to let it go and trust everyone else around me.

In a few more minutes, we were ready to go. I used my abilities to power into the air while Minsheng climbed onto Zephyr, guided by the dragon about where to sit. Roth took off with Sen on his back.

The five of us flew along, keeping fairly low to begin with. We didn't push too hard while we were out in the countryside. It was a gorgeous day, the sky blue and the world below us alive and vibrant.

If we hadn't needed to travel fast, I'd have suggested we stop to check out a couple of interesting landmarks I noticed along the way. Some old ruins, a gorgeous lake, and other beautiful places we had to pass by.

A couple of times, I checked on Minsheng to see him grinning from ear to ear as Zephyr flew. The dragon bore him easily, his large wings outstretched. Although the membranes had been damaged more than once, something magical happened when Zephyr took human form and gave them a chance to rest.

Now they were almost perfect again, although they were a lighter color where the membrane had regrown. Beside Zephyr, flying higher and looking just as graceful, was Roth. He was a strange creature I wouldn't have thought possible had he not been right in front of me. He was made of water and something entirely different.

When I looked at him, it was as if the surface of his body were rippling and moving, like the ripples and undulations of the sea, glistening and wet. Yet I when touched him, he had a strange, smooth firmness. And he was more than water, his mind phenomenal and an array of emotions projecting from him regularly.

Then there was Sen, a wood dryad, or myconid. She was shaped like a large brown mushroom, her face etched on the stalk below her cap. With long root-like feet and twig-like hands, she was the most adorable of the three, but she was also tough and capable in battle. She'd gotten me through more than one situation with her skill and size that none of the rest of us could have.

After flying for several hours and waving at folks who noticed us, we rose higher to fly over a larger town without being distracted by too many people and Minsheng grew more serious.

"You okay?" I asked Minsheng as I dropped back. "Need us to stop?"

"No. I realized how high we were and thought too much about what would happen if I fell off."

"I'd catch you if Zephyr didn't," I replied without missing a beat.

This seemed to reassure Minsheng and we flew on, although I soon grew tired of using my abilities and needed to rest. Roth carried me for an hour before the large pegasus tired as well, his body not as strong or large as Zephyr's.

I can carry you as well as Minsheng if you need me to, Zephyr offered, his voice deep but gentle. I almost rejected the offer, but I had a feeling I was going to need to rest. We still had a few hours of flying ahead of us, and I had no idea what we'd find on the other end.

I came down behind Minsheng and rested on Zephyr's back. Roth pulled into Zephyr's slipstream to get a break.

"Did the President say what this was about?" I asked.

"Not exactly. Said he was worried about some things. Asked if you'd consult and talk to his security. Nothing beyond that. I got the impression he was deliberately being vague."

"He's probably going to be surprised when he finds that

you're with me then." I grinned at the thought, knowing I often seemed to do that to people.

"Will it cause a problem?" Minsheng asked, seeming unsure of himself for the first time.

"Why would it? You have security clearance too. I made sure of it. Told the President I kept everyone at the warehouse who was part of defending it and the other mythicals informed of everything I knew."

"That's a good point." Minsheng went silent, but I got the impression something was still bothering him. I had no idea what else it could be, unless it was Chris.

"I'm sorry, Aella," Minsheng said a moment later. "I let you down."

I blinked, not sure how to respond. I was anything but let down by my Shishou.

"I invited Chris into our lives. Trusted him with everything. I should have realized he wasn't entirely on our side."

"But he was," I replied. "And he did a lot of good for us. You couldn't have stopped the rest and shouldn't blame yourself for it. Chris helped us stay safe, knowing I might be this Henera thing, and he was good at it. Without him, we wouldn't have survived everything we went through. Then he chose to pursue a different goal."

"He did more than that. Every one of his little actions was with that goal in mind. And he told them your weaknesses. Told them where you went and that Zephyr here had shown he could take human form."

"He did, but they'd have found all that out eventually either way. Chris isn't anything special in that mountain. He's just another gnome working toward Cherisse's goals.

And she's determined. If Chris made it easier on them and harder on us, it wasn't by much."

My words seemed to have an impact on Minsheng. He nodded and fell silent, but it made me worry. I'd been hurt that Chris hadn't been truthful to us, and I wasn't sure how he could believe the portals should be opened, but the gnome had saved my life. And I didn't think he truly wanted any harm to come to any of us.

It was a strange emotional place to be in, but for now, it would have to do. We couldn't worry about it. There were bigger issues to deal with than the role one gnome played.

Zephyr flew us the rest of the way. The site the President had called us to was on the edge of a mining camp in north Texas. As we came in to land, I powered off Zephyr's back, using the air to keep myself from falling and making it easier on the dragon to land with his burden.

The soldiers nearby came to attention, and one lifted a radio to report our arrival to someone inside. It wasn't long until sunset, but I could still see the building ahead clearly.

The first time I'd been here, it had been a canvas tent hastily erected over a blasting site that had revealed an ancient cavern. Now it was a complete structure built from concrete and stone. There were what looked like offices and a barracks with guard posts and a perimeter fence.

It was a serious installation, and I got the feeling only a very few select personnel went inside. Here I was striding up to the gate with a dwarf, a dragon, a pegasus, and a myconid. My life was more than strange.

CHAPTER FOUR

"Aella, Zephyr, Sen, and Roth," the President said as he motioned for me to come deeper into the building.

Only then did he notice Minsheng in the shadows beside Zephyr.

"Mr. President," I said. "This is Minsheng. He's my Shishou, my trainer, and one of my best friends. He knows a great deal about the mythical world and everything I am involved in and capable of. We both felt he should be here."

To the President's credit, he didn't blink at being introduced to someone unexpected and shook Minsheng's hand.

"Am I right in thinking you're not entirely human either?" he asked.

"Part dwarf," Minsheng replied. "On my mother's side. Chinese in every other way, but living in the US most of my life. Makes me feel as if I'm a little bit of everything."

"Well, if you've been there for Aella and can help us all understand what's going on here, you're very welcome." The President backed up, motioning for us to follow him.

I had many questions. My stomach rumbled to make it clear what one of them was. One soldier glanced at me, and the President caught his eye before looking at me and the others again.

"Peterson, have the kitchens send some food, will you? I have a feeling no one has eaten in a while, and I'm getting rather peckish myself."

Unable to help it, I grinned as the soldier hurried away and they ushered us into a large boardroom. I noticed they had pushed the table to one side to make room for the dragon. It also didn't escape my notice that all the halls, doors, and rooms were wide enough and tall enough that Zephyr could fit inside in dragon form.

Given how hard we'd struggled as Zephyr had grown, it made me warm more to the man in front of us.

"So, what's the problem?" I asked as soon as I sat down, one arm going across my stomach to stifle yet another rumble of hunger.

"Well, I don't confess to know much about this portal thing, but it doesn't seem to be shut down," the President said. "Or not entirely dormant. On top of that, we believe that we keep getting visitors. At night mostly, but it's hard to be sure."

"It seems to be concerning enough that you and I are here," I replied. "You must be fairly sure."

The President lowered his head a moment as if he were acquiescing to the observation I'd made, but as he looked at me, I saw the worry in his eyes.

"We can't take the risk if we understand all this correctly. I won't pretend that the capabilities of the elves and the mythicals you have in your care aren't scary for the general public. And for some of those in...key positions within our government."

"You want some reassurance everyone is safe?"

"I've recently been informed that your kind are far more numerous than we originally believed. Organized, powerful, and a small sect of them wishes to open a portal to a world with more. That alone is enough to have people demanding reassurances from me."

"And that's without the worry of what's on the other side of the portal."

"And with the knowledge that you are as opposed to it being opened as anyone could be. I need to...calm them."

"How can I help?" I asked, wanting to scream. Politics never seemed to end, and I couldn't get away from it.

"We'd appreciate it if you'd stay here tonight and see if you can work out what's happening. The pillars create some interesting...spikes in activity. I believe you can also feel and counteract the control of other elves if they are nearby."

"Yes," I replied. "Zephyr, Sen, and Roth are capable of that too."

"Useful. You are definitely quite the dynamic group. I am envious that you have such bonds. It seems magical in many ways." The President looked at us, taking the time to meet our eyes and smile before coming back to me. "Shall we go over what's been happening the last few days in more detail while we eat?"

I nodded, liking this man more and more. He seemed to understand that we were trying to do our best and were in a lot of ways no different, but he also had an appreciation for what we could offer.

And he understood we needed to eat. Before long, pizzas and many other foods were laid out on the board table. We dug in while several of the personnel on the base went over strange readings, video footage, and firsthand accounts of things of what had been happening during the last few days.

The more I listened to it, the more curious I became about the pillars. They were responding as if someone was trying to get through from the other side or they could feel the presence of elves on this side. It was clear they were going to need me to help them work out what.

When I was thinking about how to monitor something like that, Minsheng reached into his bag and pulled out a few devices I vaguely recognized. Some of them were tech Chris had made for us, but there were some I'd never seen before.

"These might help," he said, smiling at the President and flicking a glance in my direction.

I fought not to laugh in delight at how Minsheng must have been thinking of getting to study the pillars all along and focused instead on the rest of the problem.

It sounded as if some elves were getting close to the portal site somehow. And I could think of only one group of elves that would be consistently trying to do so. Cherisse's cult had found out about the portal. But I had no idea how they'd be getting close.

By the time we'd finished eating, they had told us everything and given us the chance to ask questions. It was very clear there was only one solution. I was going to have to be around for a night shift and see if I could figure out who was coming from where and if they were influencing the pillars.

As I made the offer, I saw relief pass over the President's face. This was what he'd hoped I'd suggest since they needed my help. It didn't sound like his job was any easier than mine. I was pretty sure it was harder. While I worked with leaders, I didn't officially lead unless there was a battle or a rescue mission. And then I was simply the first person thrown into danger.

"We're going to need to rest before then," I pointed out since we'd been awake all day. A whole night of trying to work out what was happening with the pillars was going to exhaust us if we didn't sleep first.

"I did think that might be the case. We've had an area of the barracks prepared for you. I understand you usually sleep near each other. We didn't know what Roth required, but anything you need can be found, I am sure." With this, the President got to his feet. I did the same.

It was still strange knowing who I was talking to, but I realized I had relaxed during the meeting. I felt as if I could get to know these folks and perhaps come to be friends with them. After all, we were on the same side.

The soldiers were quick to take me to the barracks, along with Minsheng and my mythicals. As we'd been informed, there was a large room with a comfy cushioned area on the floor large enough for us, and we were informed that Minsheng could use the small bunk room beside.

I requested the biggest tub of water they could manage for Roth to sleep in and a glass or pot for Sen before I moved toward the large soft area with Zephyr. It was strange to be going to bed so early, but I was tired. We'd had a full day.

The warmth of Zephyr's presence as he curled up beside me and his long bronze tail wrapping around us made the strange room feel right.

Within minutes, I slipped into sleep, my body needing it and my mind used to taking sleep whenever I could get it. It didn't last long enough, though, the time disappearing before Minsheng was there and waking us up.

I sighed, not wanting to move, but I got to my feet. Zephyr was next and then Sen, who bounded onto my shoulder. Roth came last, standing and then stepping out of the tub and splashing water around but ready to go.

It was strange to think I hadn't had these mythicals in my life for long, my mind was so comfortable with them being there. But we had a job to do: figure out what was going on with these portals.

With Minsheng and his gadgets leading the way, we went back to the main building and the pillars. It was dark and the area was lit up, with more soldiers visible than earlier as if they knew they needed them at night.

Wondering how long things had been strange, I followed Minsheng inside and got a whiff of food. Hoping they were going to feed us again, we made our way down the main hall until we reached the boardroom.

A breakfast-style meal was laid out there, and as I ate, more soldiers appeared and we were assigned people to accompany us around the place. One soldier went with Minsheng to begin gathering data, and two stuck around with me and my mythicals.

I noticed them checking Zephyr out as well as Roth,

clearly interested in the larger mythicals but not willing to say anything and draw attention to it. Stifling a smile, I finished eating.

"We usually track the perimeter and make sure the main cave is safe," the nearest soldier said. "We can take you on our route if you want, Miss Carter."

"Call me Aella," I replied, sticking my hand out. The soldier took it, grinning.

"Rick," he said, "And this is Frank."

I nodded, feeling more relaxed, then introduced them to Zephyr, Roth, and Sen. As I suspected, once they were brave enough to talk to Zephyr, it fascinated them to have a dragon in front of them.

We made our way into the corridor. The building was quieter now, most of the soldiers on duty, patrolling or heading to bed. It felt strange being the only mythicals in a base full of humans who were guarding the main portal to the elven homeworld.

Once again, I found myself drawn to it, electricity in the air and earth around it. The soldiers held back as I stared at it, the fabric cover over the entrance pulled back to reveal it.

It was a lot larger than the one Cherisse had in the mountain, and it was far more powerful. The patterns of lines and swirls on the pillars were also more intricately carved. Whoever had made this had been skilled beyond anything I'd seen before.

As I went into the room, I felt around with my abilities. Something in the center called to me, and part of me wanted to open it. Wanted to know what lay on the other side. I held back, mostly in awe.

Since the first time I'd been here, they had modified the cavern, erecting a barrier around the pillars. Nothing very high, but it was clear it marked a boundary. I walked up to it, and the soldiers followed.

As we moved nearer, something beeped on the soldiers' belts—a warning not to get too close. It was useful. I almost asked for one myself, but I could feel the raw power with my mind. My control of the surrounding air butted up against the air controlled by the pillars.

Minsheng was on the other side of the room with his gear. He was running tests, and the soldiers motioned for us to go to him. Roth joined them at the front of the group, stretching his legs and looking pleased to be along. Sen sat on his back, making faces at the soldiers. That left me to walk behind with one hand resting on Zephyr.

Are you as tempted to open this one as I am? I asked him while we walked around, the route a few hundred yards.

It has tempted me from the moment I knew we had the power to open it. To see another dragon, more elves, anything beyond this world where we're feared. But just as you couldn't risk the lives here, I do not wish to either.

We can't open it.

No, but it feels as if it wants to be open. As if something on the other side wants it open.

Him?

Maybe. He was scary, Aella. His power...I wouldn't want to face him. Tuviel and the others were hard-pressed to send him back to the elven world and close the portals on him. It was an awful time for everyone in both worlds.

I don't want to face him either. But could Cherisse be right? Could he be long dead?

Maybe. Maybe not. I don't want to take that chance.

I leaned into Zephyr as he shuddered, aware he had memories. His ancestors had fought alongside Tuviel. If she had barely been victorious, I had no idea how someone like me could win.

CHAPTER FIVE

We had circled the pillars for the fifth time when the soldiers paused near Minsheng.

My Shishou was on his feet, frowning and staring at one of his screens.

"What's wrong?" I asked, going to his side.

"There was a spike. No reason as far as I can tell, but something made this pillar react." Minsheng pointed at the pillar on his left, ahead of me.

I moved closer to it, getting right up by the barrier, and reached out with my mind. It resisted me as strongly as the area resisted any living matter in the vicinity, but I probed. It was reacting to something above it and off to one side.

Moving around the barrier until I was almost underneath it, I looked up.

"There's something up there," I said. "Could it be an animal?"

The soldiers and Minsheng came closer, the latter trying to get more readings. At the same time, I reached with my mind to find out what it was, feeling the pillars' control and trying to figure out what it fought with.

I came across something familiar and scary: the control of another elf, the earth being manipulated up there and pushed out. There was a tunnel of air, also controlled, and the signatures were familiar. I'd met these elves in a mountain a few weeks earlier.

"Cherisse has sent her elves," Zephyr said. I continued to concentrate, taking control and beginning to fill in the tunnel and swirl the air around them to make it clear I'd noticed them and planned to stop them from progressing.

"We need to work out how they got so close," I said, feeling one of them push back.

I managed to hold on, the practice I'd had lately proving useful. Zephyr led the soldiers outside and to the surface. I sent Roth and Sen with him, feeling the familiar tug in my stomach as the bond between us stretched.

Unable to move for fear of letting the elves go and allowing them to attack the pillar again, I stood my ground. It wasn't easy to fight elves I couldn't see, but I closed my eyes and focused, closing the tunnel as I blasted the elves off their feet and back.

I felt more elves attacking and gritted my teeth. They were trying to wrestle the air away from me, their control creeping into the cavern as well. Forced to fight on multiple fronts, I held my ground.

Hurry, I told Zephyr. *There are a lot of them, and I don't think I can hold them back much longer.*

We're not far away, he replied, taking flight and picking up speed, coming back toward me from somewhere overhead.

Be careful.

Always.

I exhaled and tried not to worry about him or my other mythicals as the air in the cavern was stolen from my grasp. Whoever had mastered it blasted it toward me, knocking me into the barrier.

Pain flared down my side, but the barrier held and kept worse from happening. Staying propped up against it, I tore back control of the air and considered opening a hole from where I was to them to allow me to get to them and enter the fray.

More soldiers I didn't recognize appeared at my side, aiming guns in the direction I looked. I almost laughed at how ill-equipped they were, but I had to focus as yet another fresh elf took up my challenge.

I managed to fight the elves off until a fire sprang up on one of the barriers nearby, heating the one I leaned against and forcing me to move. At the same time, the air was stolen from me.

"Put that fire out," I yelled to the nearest soldier.

As I did, the air fanned it, making it roar.

Taking a deep breath, I moved closer to the elves I could feel and forced my way back into control with every bit of power I had left. I felt them reel, one of them knocked off their feet again.

They didn't give up, just tried to brute-force their way back.

Knowing I must have looked drunk, I staggered back, feeling as if someone had smacked me in the head as they took control of the earth around the tunnel and pushed me out.

I panted and paused, letting them have that moment of victory as soldiers rushed around me.

We're here, Zephyr said. *Focus on protecting the pillars.*

Relieved, I did that, feeling him land and Sen and Roth hurtle toward me down a tunnel. They fought the elves as I did, sandwiching them between us.

Before I could push them farther back, more fires erupted, one at my feet. A soldier bowled me over, pushing both of us out of harm's way. I managed to soften our fall with a cushion of air before I scrambled to my feet.

More fires erupted, and I grew frustrated that they were using the hardest element for me to fight. Reaching deep into the earth, I sought water to bring up and douse them, but there wasn't much, the land drier than most states.

Before I could do anything else, a section of the wall a few feet up burst open and elves jumped down as I was covered in dirt and flying rocks. The air barrier around me stopped me from being seriously hurt, but several of the soldiers were less fortunate.

I noticed the tunnel was filling with a familiar-looking vapor and I took control of it, moving it toward the elves as I blasted them against the wall.

One held her ground, a woman I recognized. She had been in the sky when Zephyr and I had tried to escape from Cherisse. Another strong air elf.

The two of us stared at each other, tightening the grip we had on the surrounding air. I heard Zephyr roar a moment later and felt a stab of pain in my side, emanating from him or one of the others.

Zephyr? I thought, trying not to show what was happening to me.

No, Roth. A soldier is with him.

I'll be fine in a few minutes, Roth added.

No sooner had he finished speaking than I felt the pain lessen. It was all the relief I had before the elf nearest to me attacked. Air blasted toward me, circling and trying to disorient me as she grabbed control.

I gasped, unable to breathe as she sucked the air out of my lungs. The feeling sent me into a panic and I grabbed at the air around me. Another elf joined her, swatting my attempts away as if they were expected.

Shields up, Aella. Zephyr roared, bringing some focus to my thoughts. I did as he suggested, grabbing the air closest to me and bringing it in to form a tight barrier.

I could breathe again. At the same time, I shook the earth under the feet of the air elf, making her wobble. Before she could recover, I blasted her with more air.

Sen appeared a second later, bounding onto the shoulder of another elf and clamping down with her powerful feet at the perfect spot to make one crumple as she fired icy darts at another.

The soldiers didn't fire but they worked as a unit, fighting several of the male elves hand to hand until someone appeared with tranquilizer guns. The air elves tried to blast the darts and weapons away, but I took control of the air and held onto it.

The Amcika elves fell unconscious, feathery darts sticking out of their limbs or torsos. Zephyr's vapor had an effect as well. A couple of elves were out cold before Roth came running through the tunnel, no longer in as much pain.

Realizing we had defeated them, the rest of the elves broke off, hitting all of us hard with air and making the whole cavern rumble and quake as they powered upward and through the tunnel.

I didn't hesitate to go after them. As I did, I noticed the tunnel still had some vapor in it. Zephyr's breath weapon was extremely potent.

Hoping the fire elf ahead of me didn't get any ideas and ignite it, I flew through the hole they'd made, trying to pull the air around the retreating elves and trip them. It only worked on one elf, but the young woman fell to her knees. Before she could get up, I grabbed the next pocket of vapor and wrapped it around her head.

She slumped, out cold as I flew out of the tunnel. I felt Zephyr in the sky nearby rather than seeing him, the night sky dark and overcast. Any elves who had been ahead of me scattered, and I couldn't see well enough to chase them. Instead, I landed as Zephyr did, noticing he had an elf hanging from his front claws.

A soldier came out of the tunnel behind me and didn't hesitate to trank the female elf and the dragon's captive. Zephyr let out a chuckle.

"You'll want to get the elves restrained swiftly," I said, noticing the pain where Roth had been hurt was not gone and I had bruises of my own.

The soldiers nodded, working together to take the elves away. I didn't move, so drained and exhausted from the fight that I couldn't think straight.

Once again I'd come close to being defeated, the lengths

the elves were willing to go to get what they wanted taking me by surprise.

Are you okay? Zephyr asked, coming closer and looking at me.

I think so.

You're hurt.

Yeah. I got air-shoved into a barrier and then almost set alight.

That's a new one. A singed you is less appealing. I'm not sure I want my girlfriend to smell smoky like dragon food.

You don't breathe fire. You're a paralyzing dragon.

I still like my food burned and charcoal-based. The windswept hair look suits you, although maybe not because other elves have been knocking you around.

Tell me about it. Normally it's me air-blasting people.

Zephyr and I grinned, then I realized the soldiers were looking at us as if they were waiting for us to give orders or explain. Anything but look at each other with goofy expressions.

When I went to move, I realized how much I hurt. I was going to have some epic bruises.

"I'll close this tunnel, but you might want to widen the perimeter of the compound and patrol the entire thing," I said to the nearest soldier as I tried to walk.

Roth came forward and tucked his body against mine, giving me something to drape my arm over and support my weight. Grateful for all three of my mythicals, I continued toward the tunnel. We'd worked together in a new way, all three of them coming to my rescue. It made me adore them more.

Zephyr didn't fit down the tunnel, so he was forced to

accompany the soldiers the long way, but I made my way inside and closed it as I went. I took my time, leaning into Roth and listening to Sen as she chattered, delighted with being somewhere different.

The pain faded as I focused on moving the earth around. I packed it tighter than it had been, making sure it wouldn't be as easy to get through a second time. I wondered if there was a good way to stop something like this from happening with so little warning again.

Defending a place like this would require a large group of earth elementals to fortify it against attack, and I knew only one place where I could find enough I trusted—the Sanctuary.

As soon as the tunnel was blocked, I surveyed the cavern's interior. The barriers were scorched in several places, and there was a mess of foamy sludge where fire extinguishers had been used. The human race didn't stand a chance if elves brought war to this world.

When the nearest soldier realized I was done, he ushered me toward the boardroom, mentioning a debrief. Sighing and wishing I could rest, I made my way to the meeting.

You should tell them you're hurt, Zephyr said.

What would that change? They'll fuss over me and then ask me if I can handle the debrief anyway, and I'll have to go because they can't do this without the skills and wisdom we have.

Yes. Wisdom we have. I can go to it for you.

My mouth fell open as I realized he had a point. I'd forgotten that he could talk to them for me.

I'm sorry, I said, knowing it wasn't right for me to overlook him.

It's okay. We need to take care of you sometimes too.

Zephyr's concern and warmth made me feel better as I went to find a medic. While the small burns I had were bandaged and my rib cage was checked, I listened to the debrief via Zephyr. From the images Sen sent me, there was shock that I had sent Zephyr instead of coming.

It didn't take long for the dragon to remind everyone we shared a bond and that having an elf's mythical present wasn't far from having the elf. This made Minsheng grin and the President pause, but he dropped the matter and let the meeting go ahead.

When the food arrived and I was given the all-clear by the medic, I joined them.

"Right," the President said as I walked in. "That settles what happened tonight and what we lost. Now, none of us are leaving until I have some way of making sure it doesn't happen again."

I almost laughed when everyone turned to me as if I had the answer.

"There are some elves at the Sanctuary who should be able to fortify the place and help defend it the same way I did," I said as I went to the table and picked up a donut. "I'll need to talk to their council about who they're willing to spare, however. They're likely to want to make sure they can defend themselves, too."

"Thank you, Aella," he said as I sat down. I winced as I jolted my side, grateful the painkillers I'd been given were taking the edge off.

"You're going to need both humans and elves patrolling. This cult isn't fooling around. They tried to kill me today, and if I hadn't been stronger and had Zephyr, Sen, and Roth, they might have succeeded."

I closed my mouth with a snap, the conversation that came after my words fading into the background as I realized what I'd said.

They'd tried to kill me. Almost succeeded. But I was supposed to be the key they needed. Had something changed, or had it been a mistake?

A wave of warmth from Zephyr brought me back to reality and made it clear he'd heard my thoughts, but it wasn't the time to discuss it. Something had changed; I was sure of it. But what?

CHAPTER SIX

As the sun started its descent in the sky, I walked out of the compound by the portal, tired and achy but ready to head back to the Sanctuary.

After the fight, we'd stayed up to ensure the elves we hadn't captured would not come back, then gotten some rest.

The medic had insisted on checking my wounds again. I had a deep shade of purple down one side, but being elven came with the perk of healing faster than most. I was going to be fine in a week or so, and mostly pain-free sooner.

Still, I wasn't in perfect health. It made me wary as I looked at the sky and the surrounding countryside. Out there somewhere were some pissed-off elves, and they'd consider me an excellent target if they found me out in the middle of nowhere and drained.

With that in mind, we planned for me not to use my abilities to fly and didn't take Minsheng with us. He could get back to the Sanctuary another way when he was ready.

It wasn't ideal for me to leave him behind, and he'd shown concern, but I'd seen the look in his eyes when one of the scientists at the compound had offered to let him look at data and other information on their computers. He was happy here.

I used my abilities to lift onto Zephyr's back so I wouldn't have to climb and settled into the most comfortable position I could. Zephyr waited for the pain of moving to subside, then leaped into the air, his wings taking over a moment later and lifting us higher. Sen and Roth followed, the myconid grinning broadly.

It was going to be a long afternoon, but I wanted to enjoy the flight despite the threat. There was something deeply satisfying and thrilling about flying.

Time seemed to fall away as I took in the view and thought about how much our lives had changed. We'd come a long way, but I was looking forward to feeling safe and at peace again. We'd had snatches and moments, a few days here or there when there were no problems and we could fly and explore together and talk about going on an epic vacation.

Now, however, we had to fly to the Sanctuary yet again. We needed to persuade some of them to come to an unknown location and trust a group of people who would have happily killed them a year ago, all because there was another group of people who wanted to open a portal to hell and doom everyone.

And at any point, the same group could attack us. Fun times.

Relax, Zephyr said. *We're flying high enough that only the air elementals would reach us, and we've shown we can trounce those.*

I sighed. Zephyr was right, but not worrying was easier said than done.

The hours ticked by as we flew, the sky changing as we went farther west. We passed through a rain shower and had to fly lower to avoid the large clouds that bore it, unable to get over it and needing to see.

We were coming out of it and beginning to climb again when a gust knocked me sideways. I almost fell off Zephyr, and pain flared as the bruised muscles on that side were stretched.

Elves, Zephyr said.

Letting out a frustrated growl, I centered myself on his back and gripped him tighter.

Want me to fly up and get rid of most of them?

I wanted to say no and to insist on taking them all on and teaching them a lesson, but Zephyr was already doing it, putting more distance between us and the elves.

Before he could get very far, one of the three elves in the air with us blasted a gust at Sen and Roth. The myconid hadn't been prepared for it, the pegasus being higher in the air and farther from danger.

She fell, squealing the whole way.

I propelled myself off Zephyr and flew toward her. She was the only one of us who couldn't fly and I wouldn't let her fall, no matter what happened or how much it hurt.

Zephyr let out a roar so loud it made my ears ring.

Eyes locked on Sen as she fell and mind trying to calm her and tell her I was going to catch her, I pushed as hard as I dared.

Another blast hit me, knocking me sideways and spinning me until I wasn't sure which way was up and could only feel Sen thanks to the bond. By the time I was heading toward her again, we were lower, and the distance between us had increased.

I need you to keep them from hitting me, I told Zephyr and Roth, desperate to get to Sen.

She was trying to spread out and slow her to fall, but she was tiny, and I was far larger. I was having to fight hard to close the gap, and the pain in my side was growing. It would be hurting the others too.

Elves came into focus on the ground as it came closer. I could feel Zephyr and Roth following, and I had to hope they were protecting me from behind as Sen came within a meter of my outstretched hand.

When I was close enough, I wrapped a hand around her middle and brought her in close to my jacket as I tried to slow. She clung to me, nestling in tight and flooding me with her relief.

If we'd been higher, I'd have taken my time to slow us, not wanting to hurt her, but we were close to the ground, so I had to do everything I could to slow and lift. As it was, I had too little height left.

When we crash-landed in the trees, pain flared in my body. I managed to cushion myself with vines and slow down enough with air to come to a stop.

I didn't move, one hand still protectively over Sen. She had squealed again as we landed and bumped into stuff.

You okay? I asked her as I tried to stand, more pain flaring in my side.

Yes. Aella hurt, she replied.

Relief flooded through me as I realized the pain my mythicals were feeling was mine, not theirs. I could cope with being the one in pain. Admittedly, I was worried about the amount that would transfer through our bond, and I tried to dampen it.

I didn't get very far before I was hit in the chest with a blast of air, knocking me off my feet again. The vines around me sprang to life, grabbing my limbs and pinning me down.

Rather than fighting the vines, I fought for control of them, hitting back and hitting hard. My pain fueled my anger until I was in control again and getting back to my feet.

I moved outward with the vines as Zephyr and Roth landed and came toward me. The air elves followed them, and everyone paused.

"I'm not going anywhere with you," I said in as loud and confident a voice as I could manage.

It was met with a laugh from the woman who had blasted Sen off Roth's back.

"Don't think so much of yourself," she said as she stepped closer. "We don't need you anymore, but we won't waste an opportunity to get you out of our way."

Before she'd finished speaking, I felt her trying to wrestle control of the air from me, her strength surprising. But I was ready and waiting, and I twisted out of her grasp and blasted her off her feet.

She hit the ground with a *whooomph*, triggering several more elves to attack.

Not wanting to run the risk of being overwhelmed, I rocked the ground outward to knock everyone off their feet while growing the plants in the area in a protective circle. With that done, I powered into the air to get out of range of as many of the elves as I could before they recovered.

It wasn't easy, and I could feel the elves trying to take control of anything and everything to stop me.

Come closer to me, Zephyr said as Roth flew toward an air elf trying to follow us and attacked her with a blast of water and a kick from his hooves.

I wasn't going to argue since the large dragon could not only help keep Sen and me in the air but give me some respite. My entire side was ablaze with pain, and they'd be feeling it too.

As I moved toward him, Zephyr came up from underneath, catching me and lifting me in one swoop. I paused on his back to allow the pain to fade, gratitude filling me for the support I had.

Despite resting physically, I knew I couldn't in any other way as Zephyr and Roth continued to climb with me.

Just keep getting higher, I said to everyone. If these air elves were going to take me on, they were going to have to risk everything.

Roth pulled back from the air elf near him, coming up toward us, but I saw him wobble as an elf nearby hit him with air. I blasted the air near him and formed a barrier of air around his body, adding to his slipstream as well as giving extra lift beneath his wings.

He came closer, able to make some headway, and I blasted at the elf behind him. Another elf tried to hit Zephyr with something but the dragon banked out of the way, keeping me stable and in place as he moved.

As we rose, the elves on the ground were no longer a threat, but there were still some in the air, and they weren't giving up. They flew after us, trying to knock me off Zephyr or attack Roth as the weaker member of the group.

Nothing they did worked. I concentrated on holding air around us and keeping us climbing. I blasted at them a few times to discourage them, but I didn't need to do much more. We were safe, and there was nothing they could do about it.

Eventually they dropped back, but I noticed they watched us travel for some time. I didn't move from Zephyr's back, exhausted and terrified that there might be more elves waiting for us.

Rest, Zephyr said. *And keep Sen safe. We'll get to the Sanctuary and see what they can do to heal you.*

I wasn't going to argue with that. I was pretty sure I had fresh bruises after hitting the bushes so hard, and I'd made my previous injury worse.

The events of the last twenty-four hours didn't bode well for our future. The elves didn't care if I was alive anymore, and that was worrying. If they didn't need Zephyr and me, then they'd found an alternative. And I was pretty sure that was a bad thing.

But it also begged questions. What was happening in the mountain? Did they have a team of people? Was that portal open? Or was there something different about the portal in Texas?

With so few answers, there was nothing I could do but worry and wait. And make it clear to the council that we might need to step in and do something sooner rather than later. We couldn't allow Cherisse and her elves to continue this.

It was a relief when the Sanctuary came into sight. The great elven city nestled on one side of the mountains, at one with nature but more beautiful than the natural world could craft. It never failed to take my breath away.

I stayed on Zephyr's back after he landed near the border, always polite enough not to cross the boundary in the air. The guards patrolling the edge sensed something was wrong. One took a glance at me and scurried off.

"We didn't expect to see you so soon," the dwarf said as he slid down the ladder from the guard post.

"I didn't expect to be back this soon, but I must seek the Sanctuary's aid once more. Convene the council as soon as possible to talk more about the pillars and tell them I will be there as soon as I have sought medical attention from Orthelo."

The guard nodded, letting out a whistle. A hawk flew off the guard tower and toward the center of the city. I raised my eyebrows; this explained how they'd always gotten messages to the council quickly, but I dared not ask.

Zephyr bore me to the hospital. As a healer, Orthelo had helped Zephyr and me on more than one occasion. Although he wasn't a doctor, he knew a lot about mythicals.

When we found him, tending to the animals as always, Daisy was with him.

They rushed over as I used my abilities to get off Zephyr's back. I winced as I landed and heard a soft rumble from my dragon. Roth came to my side, letting me lean on him, and Sen wriggled out of my jacket and jumped onto the winged horse's back.

I didn't utter a word, just lifted the edge of my shirt so they could see the bruising and moved my jacket so the bandages over the burns were evident.

Daisy gasped and helped me toward the hut where Orthelo performed miracles.

CHAPTER SEVEN

When I made my way into the council chamber, they were all there waiting. Thankfully, someone had thought to lay out a meal. They weren't sitting at tables but on soft cushions on a blanket in the center of an open area.

Sierrathen got up and came to me, Vestan following.

"We hear you were hurt." The gentle-voiced elf offered me her arm.

I nodded. I felt better after all the salves and aid Orthelo and Daisy had given me as well as strong painkillers, but moving still hurt, and I could tell it was taking its toll on Zephyr, Sen, and Roth.

Despite the pain, we moved to the cushions and sat down. We were hungry, and it was a good idea to inform the council of what was going on while we ate.

It didn't take long for me to explain what had happened and what I'd found at the portal. And they were bright enough to work out where I was going with my story.

"You want our help?" Vestan asked. "To protect it."

I nodded, not seeing any point in hiding it.

"They can't defend that portal alone. The elves can walk all over them and tunnel in from all sorts of angles. They need elves and more than just me."

"Then we will have to send some, but I do not think we can force anyone," Vestan replied.

"I would not ask you to command anyone into danger. They have no problem killing those in their way."

"And that seems to include you now," Sierrathen added, picking up on the only thing I hadn't mentioned.

"It does."

"I confess this worries me more than anything else you have told us." Ronan lowered his head toward me, the centaur sign of respect.

I returned the gesture, grateful for his care. It worried me too, and for more than one reason.

Over the next hour, we talked about all the possible reasons the elves were acting the way they were and what could be done about it. We also talked about the two elves who had sought refuge in the Sanctuary, and it was agreed that I would talk to them. I hoped they would respond better to me because I had spoken to them more than once and been the catalyst for them leaving Cherisse and her cult.

After insisting I needed to rest, the council meeting ended. Once again, I marveled at the way things had changed between the Sanctuary and me. They trusted me, and we felt more like allies than we had in the past.

You have grown in power, and it is clear you are the Henera, Zephyr said as he encouraged me onto his back so he could carry me to the lodge. It was dark outside when we left the cave network, but Gwaelon came to us as we emerged.

"Good evening, Aella. May I accompany you to your abode for the night?" he asked.

I didn't object, pretty sure this was his way of letting me know he had something to say. Whatever it was, I trusted Gwaelon. He had our best interests at heart.

As we walked, he talked about inconsequential things: the latest weather patterns, another bet on my skills with his brother, the water master, and the hunt for the final artifact from the great elven masters of old. I'd described the belt to him and the fire master the last time I was in the Sanctuary.

As soon as we were inside the lodge, Gwaelon got serious. I found myself growing concerned.

"Orthelo came to me after doing what he could for you. I'm worried about you and what they're intending."

"That makes a lot of us."

"I think we need to gather more intel. Ruehnar and I have discussed the possibility of me becoming a spy and going to the mountain in Mexico you described."

I shook my head. There was no way something like that was safe.

"We need to know if they've opened that portal."

Exhaling, I frowned. Gwaelon had a point, but it was an incredibly dangerous thing to suggest. They could easily decide to kill him, or worse, torture him, or send him into the field around the pillars and let them tear him apart.

I shuddered as I thought of how it had felt to be in that field with multiple elves fighting it to keep me alive. It had hurt, and it had taken a lot of my power to withstand.

"I wanted you to know that we were considering it."

"Please don't do it yet," I replied. "Not unless we think

it's necessary, and not without me giving you as much information as possible first."

"I won't deny I was hoping you'd offer. I would go in blind if I thought it was needed to stop those portals being opened, but I would rather go prepared."

"If it comes to it, I will do what I can to help you."

"Thank you, Aella. You are truly everything we hoped you'd be. I shall rest more easily knowing I do not have to venture into that darkness to prevent catastrophe just yet and will have your guidance when I do." Gwaelon shuddered as he got up, making me realize there was something very emotional about his determination to stop the portals from being opened.

"Do you know what lies on the other side?" I asked.

"No. Not first hand," Gwaelon looked into the distance, clearly remembering something. "But my father...he was a lot older by the time he met my mother. He was there in the great war. Saw what destruction could be wrought and how many could be hurt. It haunted him."

"I'm sorry," I said, wanting to hug the water elf, his eyes taking on a shine that showed he was close to tears.

"It's not your fault. I'm grateful you're here now. I still don't know what we're going to see in our lifetimes, but if there's a chance you can stop this from ever being a possibility again, I'll stand by your side every step of the way."

Gwaelon did the very thing I'd wanted to and came to me for a hug, although he was careful not to hurt me further.

"I will let you rest, but should the time come, we should talk more."

Not sure what to say in the face of such conviction and

desire to do his part, I simply let him go. This was proving to be a challenge of a new type. Before when I'd been fighting, it had been easy to feel as if it were us against them. Mythicals being hunted and murdered by humans. But this was different.

This was beliefs and opinions taken so far that everyone forgot we all wanted the same thing: to live in peace with the people we cared about.

And everyone had a different take on how to do it. But the worst part was who had to choose. Everyone was looking to Zephyr and me.

Could we make this decision? How would we know if we were right?

We won't be right, Zephyr said as he curled up to sleep. *No one is ever entirely right. We do our best and hope it's enough. You and I, Sen and Roth, we've been given power and a bond others don't have. The world, a deity, nature, whatever gave it to us, it's in our hands.*

I slowly lay down beside him, trying to avoid hurting myself and struggling to process what he was saying.

We were a lot more powerful than most. I'd seen it as a blessing in the past, but I wasn't so sure. Part of me didn't want this responsibility anymore.

We'll take it one day at a time and do what seems right at every point. Apologize and try to put it right if we screw up. All we can do.

I leaned into Zephyr, grateful I had him in my life. His wisdom and calmness had seen me through many things, and I had hope we'd get through everything else we faced together.

Sleeping wasn't easy with the pain in the background,

and it was clear I wasn't the only one of us struggling with it. Zephyr kept swishing the end of his tail, Roth's hooves clicked in his tub, and Sen couldn't seem to settle in the small pool of water the lodge had prepared for her.

The hours ticked by. We did our best until I gave up, as rested as I was going to be.

That was another difficulty in our lives. We never slept well in the middle of a situation or problem we had not solved, and this was no different. The only gain had been time to regenerate the power we'd used and to heal more.

Whatever Orthelo had done to me had helped a lot. Once I'd worked out the stiffness, I encouraged everyone else to get up, and we went in search of breakfast.

I didn't get very far before I noticed most of the council heading toward the area of the city where the newer elves and mythicals were lodged. Sierrathen caught my eye and indicated I should follow.

Hoping it wouldn't take long, I went with the council, curious. Of course, I'd seen them all in the Sanctuary before—they didn't hide in the council chambers—but this wasn't normal behavior.

We made our way through the houses to a smaller one near the edge of the city. Two elves were sitting together, eating breakfast in the sunlight. Two elves I recognized. The two from Cherisse's cult.

The moment they noticed us, the atmosphere changed. They sat upright, their backs stiff, the food forgotten.

"Please don't be alarmed," Sierrathen said, moving to stand at the front of the group. "You're not in any trouble."

"Then why the small army?" the air elf asked, her eyes narrowing.

"The council is struggling with something we thought you might be able to help with. They've all come with me so you don't have to repeat yourselves. And Aella, Zephyr, Sen, and Roth are our greatest allies and will be our greatest asset should anything evil befall our world. Perhaps we could join you for breakfast?"

This seemed to relax them a little, although I was sure they were still uneasy. Hoping to help, I was the first to step forward. I bowed as a centaur might and sat down on the edge of a nearby wall, pretty sure I wouldn't be able to get lower and up again without hurting myself.

While I was more inclined to trust these elves as time passed and they remained functioning members of the Sanctuary, I wasn't about to let them see how hurt I was. Zephyr came close to me, but Sen bounded onto the small table between them and helped herself to a muffin.

I grinned. Her greed broke the tension. Within minutes, everyone was sitting on blankets or chairs, Martyl had perched on the wall near me, and food was being brought.

My fear of missing breakfast was allayed by the spread put out before us. I wouldn't go hungry, and neither would anyone else. More interested in listening at this point, I focused on eating and was grateful when Ronan held out platters of food for me so I didn't have to move or risk showing my pain.

"So, what have you all come to ask us?" the air elf asked, acting as the spokesperson for the pair.

"Recently, elves from your old order attacked a rumored portal site. Aella happened to be there." Vestan glanced my way before continuing. "They tried to kill her. This concerns us."

The air elf nodded but didn't reply.

"It has become clear that Cherisse no longer feels she needs Aella, Zephyr, or anyone else."

"And you want to know if we have any idea why?"

"If there's anything you can tell us that might explain this change in actions. Last we knew, Cherisse needed Zephyr and Aella. Now she doesn't appear to."

The earth elemental who had guarded me nodded and leaned forward.

"Another elf came into her power. It was surprisingly efficient, and she was one of the missing links we needed. Cherisse has her training with the strongest elves of each type to destroy the pillars. It helped that Aella attempted it the way she did."

Suddenly all eyes were on me, and I froze. It seemed I had screwed something up or given Cherisse more than I'd realized.

"When Aella went into the zone the pillars controlled, she focused on one, letting the elves with her focus more on keeping her alive. It almost worked, though she was weaker than normal."

Everyone seemed to understand now, concern filling their faces.

"So, Cherisse thinks this elf can go into the force field alone, break one pillar while many others fight to protect her, and do the same with each one."

I frowned. It was a good strategy, and it was one I'd come up with. I'd handed them the answer they needed.

"I take it that's not what was attempted before?" Sierra-then asked.

"No. It was believed that all the pillars had to be

attacked at once, but it's clear that isn't the case. It's also clear that not all the elves have to be in the zone at the same time. In short, it's more possible than it's ever been."

There was a silence in answer to this statement, everyone realizing the same thing. This had gotten far worse. If they had the right people in place, they could open any portal at any point.

"How ready are they to make the attempt?" I asked when no one else spoke. I could feel their panic rising.

"They're not there yet, or at least, they weren't when we left. The elf with the fire gift is young and still in training, but as soon as she's ready..." The air elemental's voice trailed off, her eyes fixed on me.

"Thank you," I said as I slowly got to my feet. There was a similar reaction from some of the others, Ronan bowing to the Amcika elves as Vestan helped Sierrathen to her feet.

"I've heard enough," I added to the council. "It's clear we must also train and act."

Without another word, I walked away from the group. I was still hurting and feeling so many emotions. In my attempt to learn more and dupe Cherisse, I had given her a way to open the portals.

We had no idea that would happen. You can't blame yourself, Zephyr said.

I knew he was right, but it didn't matter. My actions had led to it, although I had been trying to survive. It didn't help to know that they might have figured it out on their own eventually. But one thing I did know. I had to put it right, and I had to stop Cherisse once and for all.

CHAPTER EIGHT

Sitting on Zephyr's back, ready to head out again, I tried to stay calm. After speaking to the two refugees, Sierrathen had called a meeting of all the elves and informed them of the danger and the desire to do something about it.

A mixed group had volunteered to protect the portal in Texas, and the council had selected the best of the bunch. Two masters had volunteered, and part of me had been enthusiastic about the idea of having the levelheaded elves in the group, but the council had rightly stopped them.

Instead, the only elf I knew the name of in the group was Seth. I wasn't expecting him to be the voice of reason. I could only hope they would all get along with the humans. None of them had much experience, but I was going to act as their escort and liaison for now.

The President had thanked me for finding aid and allies. We'd agreed to set out as soon as possible to ensure the safety of the portal. Although they had seen no elves nearby and Minsheng had been fine last night, none of us thought it was wise to leave it unattended for another night.

With the twelve elves selected, Zephyr, Sen, Roth, and I in the skies, and Daisy and Holfin as extra tech support and hands, we made an interesting group. They were traveling together in three large cars. Zephyr, Sen, Roth, and I were going to act as escorts and fly along with them.

Given that we'd run into Cherisse's elves last time, I didn't want to take the chance that they wouldn't notice the elves and let them through. I was the best defense they had.

As soon as everyone was ready, Zephyr lifted into the air. It jolted me, sending a stab of pain, but I was getting better. I was determined to finish this mission.

I used my abilities to boost Zephyr and Roth. Sen tucked herself into my jacket again rather than fly with Roth. It wasn't what she wanted, but we had to keep her safe.

Once we were in the air, I felt a lot better. We were doing something and ensuring that Cherisse didn't have all the cards. There was still more to do, but that was better than nothing.

The convoy moved more slowly than we could. We had to circle back occasionally and check that everyone was still all together and not being followed.

It was tiring, but Zephyr was handling it well. I worried about Roth. He preferred being in the water to the air, but there was no other way to get to Texas. Moving more of my power to him, I helped him fly and keep up.

Not wanting to wear myself out, I did no more than I had to. If there was going to be trouble, I needed to make sure I had as much power as possible. I wouldn't be able to outfly everyone if they hit the convoy. They'd need me to defend them and keep everyone safe.

I also didn't feel like I could relax. This wasn't a flight where I could take it easy and enjoy the view or dream of traveling in far-off places. This was my responsibility, and I couldn't let anyone down.

Thankfully, the time slipped by, and the only stop we had to make was a toilet break. I picked up snacks at the same time, not wanting to take any chances on the second half of the trip and feeling peckish again and then having to get the group on the road.

Lunch had been grabbed in the middle of preparations, and I hated going without food. I was pretty sure Zephyr felt the same, so I asked for plenty from the store and we wolfed it down before we got into the air again.

I tried not to laugh at his antics as I checked on Roth. He was tired, and he was going to need a rest when we got to the site.

I need to spend some time in the sea, Roth said. *It does something nothing else can.*

Not sure what to say, I promised we'd go there as soon as we could. We would have gone right away if it was safe to do so, but we had work to do.

Part of me considered releasing his bond and letting him go back to the sea where I'd found him, but he was happy with us, and I didn't want him to think I was cutting him loose at the first sign of trouble and weakness from him. It wasn't right for me to treat him like that.

The second half of our journey went more swiftly, my focus more on helping Roth than on the convoy. None of us spoke much, feeling the pain I was in and the stress and pressure of our lives. I could only hope that Minsheng had found something useful about the portals that would make our trip worthwhile.

The dwarf was outside waiting for us when we arrived. I smiled, and his grin grew when he saw his sister and other elves he recognized. I noticed the soldiers weren't as happy to see a convoy of elves, but they didn't make a fuss when Zephyr and I landed beside them.

I powered myself off his back and stood in front of everyone just in case.

"Please inform the President that I've brought a group of skilled elves from the Sanctuary to aid in defending the portal, as well as two of the most skilled Sanctuary guards to act as their command," I said as the nearest soldiers stepped forward.

They raised their eyebrows and looked at the mythicals behind me as they got out of the car, but they saluted before they went inside.

Hoping everything would be received with the correct intent, I helped everyone unearth their luggage and take it to the barracks. We were moving the last load over when the President appeared.

I stopped in shock. I'd assumed he'd left after the danger from the elves attacking, but he was still here.

"Aella, thank you so much," the President said as he came over to shake my hand. "Why don't you introduce me to everyone, and we'll see about getting them all settled in and a plan put together before nightfall."

There was no more encouragement needed. The elves

came over, none of them having a clue who the man before them was but noticing I'd been greeted warmly.

I quickly ushered everyone inside, promising to come soon, then focused on Roth. He was standing near the barracks and had been since we landed. He wasn't looking good.

Thankfully, one of the soldiers who was still nearby was responsible for the barracks. I instructed him to fetch a tub of water for Roth and let the pegasus bask in it for a while to give him space and time to rest.

It wasn't ideal and I was sure I wouldn't enjoy being apart from Roth, but he wasn't as ready for this life as we needed him to be yet. Zephyr had grown up like this and Sen could always snuggle up in my jacket if everything grew too much, but Roth was suddenly having to fly to all sorts of places.

Tired but needing to make this work, I made my way across the outside space to the main building. Before I got through the door, Sen wriggled in my jacket.

Sen go to Roth, she said. I considered trying to persuade her to stay with me, but it was better for Roth to have a companion. I could feel a strange emotion from him I couldn't place.

Helping Sen down, I sent my warmest feelings of affection to both of them. Things were hard, and they were my family.

Feeling torn, I went into the main building.

I never got as far as the meeting the elves were in. Minsheng and Daisy were still out in the corridor. The expression on Minsheng's face made it clear he had something to tell or ask me.

When I went over to him and Daisy, I saw one of Chris' old tools in his hands. I lifted my eyebrows.

"I need to show you something," Minsheng said. "The portal is doing bizarre things."

We need to be in two places, I said to Zephyr since we were supposed to be in the meeting with the elves.

Go with Minsheng. I'll go keep the elves and soldiers in check. I have a feeling a big scary-looking dragon will have enough of an impact to keep them all in order.

I smiled but felt bereft. All my mythicals were off doing something else, and it felt strange to not have any of them at my side. I took a deep breath and tried not to panic at the tug in my stomach.

On top of everything, I was tired. Being in pain was draining me, but I was going to have to push through. I had something to see.

As I headed to the pillar room with Minsheng and Daisy, I made sure the latter didn't get too close, feeling a difference.

"Oh, that's worse than before," Minsheng said. As he spoke, the barriers shook, then calmed.

The same thing happened a moment later, but this time I was ready to pick up on it, my mind feeling for the control in the room. It expanded a couple of inches from the center before going back to normal.

While I stood there, the device Minsheng had set to record showed it doing the same thing three more times. It then went back to normal, not fluctuating anymore.

"I think something is changing the influence of the pillars," Minsheng said, picking up on what I was feeling.

Nodding, I moved closer and waited for it to do it again, but it didn't.

"How often does it change?" I asked.

"It varies, but it's roughly consistent each day."

"Consistent?" I whirled to look at him. What could consistently make the pillars fluctuate when there was nothing living and powerful close enough except me?

"It's not exact, but roughly the same time each day, there are three separate sessions where the pillars fluctuate several times. It varies how much and how powerfully, but something is happening, and I'm not sure what."

"Leave it with me," I replied, thinking.

I closed my eyes, concentrating on the portal. Something about it was different. All the previous times I'd interacted with this site or the one in the mountain, I had focused on the pillars. It had all been about trying to break them or pretending to. It was time to find out what the portal felt like.

My mind reached beyond the pillars to the portal. The pillars resisted my probing, making it hard for me to get to the portal to test anything, but I pushed through. This wasn't supposed to be easy, or any elf could open the portals.

I was on the edge of the section that made up the portal when I felt it trying to draw my mind in as if it wanted me to connect. Unable to help it, I did so and felt the power of another elf.

Something reached out to me and grabbed me, something powerful and hungry. I could feel the power being pulled out of me as whatever it was came close to the portal.

At the same time, the room shook, and the glowing lines on the pillars and portal grew brighter. Yanking back, I severed the connection, realizing as I did that I was panting hard and my head was swimming.

What happened? Zephyr asked. *It was as if something was trying to take over our bond and pull everything you were away from us.*

Yeah. Something...or someone on the other side. I shuddered at the thought of something wanting to get at us. Had that been what happened?

Minsheng and Daisy rushed to my side, concern on their faces. I tried not to panic them and straightened up, but as I did, my vision blurred again. It forced me to bend over and focus on my breathing.

"Did something on the other side try to pull you in?" Minsheng asked.

"Not exactly. It was as if it were...checking me out. Trying to work out who and what I was. I was pulled closer as if I weren't in control of the connection." I stopped talking, realizing I was rambling as I tried to explain it.

After taking several deeper breaths, I explained again. The nearby soldiers left and fetched the President. In the end, I had to tell the story three times, each time gaining more clarity and surety about what I'd felt.

There had been another elf on the other side of the portal, and they had connected with me. I didn't like how it had made me feel. Something about them had been brutal.

"Does it mean they can open the portals from the other side?" the President asked when I finished again.

"I don't think so. It was as if whoever I connected with

wanted *me* to open it. Was trying to...persuade me to open it."

"That's not good news."

"No. It's not. But it's not bad news either." Minsheng held up the instrument in his hands. "I got good readings. Whoever connected with you, they're not the one who caused the normal anomaly. I'm seeing signatures of a sort."

"So, there are multiple elves on the other side?" The President looked more concerned.

"It's highly likely. And it means that whoever is on the other side, there's no guarantee they're a threat collectively. Even if one of them is a problem, many might be fine."

I exhaled at Minsheng's words. He had a point, but it was still a huge risk to consider anything on the other side.

"Whatever is on the other side, it's clear we need to be wary of it. None of the elves here should get too close to the portal except to defend it," I said.

"I think we all agree on that."

"And in the meantime, I'll try to work out who or what connected with me, and we'll see if there are multiple elves on the other side. Maybe we can communicate and find out what's going on."

This seemed to pacify everyone, and we were all ushered back into the boardroom to continue talking about the future defense of the portal. It was needed. I hated to think what might have happened if Cherisse or one of her fanatics had connected with something as I had done. Would it have led to the portals being opened?

CHAPTER NINE

The dawn was stunning over the wide-open land to one side of the compound. Zephyr, Sen, Roth, and I had snuck away to get some fresh air, and we were sitting on a small hill, watching the sun come up. Although we'd all slept, and Roth had recovered in the saltwater bath the soldiers had made for him, none of us had much energy.

Overnight, little had happened, all the elves getting settled in and beginning their first round of sentry duty with the soldiers. The night watch coming back to the barracks had woken us. So far, it was good news, but I wasn't at ease.

It felt like something big was coming, and I couldn't help but think of whatever, or whoever, I had connected to on the other side of the portal. It made me shudder and my heart race every time I thought about what it had been doing to me. I was worse to know it had been felt by my bonded mythicals to a lesser degree.

The sun coming up on another day brought hope with it, however. We found ourselves getting up and going back

to the compound, ready to face the day and whatever challenges it brought.

I wanted to get back to the warehouse if I could and
train, but I also wanted to see if I could find out what was
on the other side of that portal and if they were trying to
break through.

But first, we needed food.

I found Minsheng in the mess hall, his device in his
hands. It was showing the portal was quiet, static, and
nothing was happening yet.

"In about half an hour," Minsheng said as he noticed me
looking at the readings. "First time each day."

"I should be in there," I replied as we all got food and sat
back down.

Despite not draining my abilities the previous day, I
was hungry and the others were too. I couldn't focus on
the food, however. My eyes were drawn to the device on
the table every few seconds.

The half-hour seemed to drag by, but I was eating my
last mouthful when it changed, the number on the screen
flicking upward. We got to our feet and rushed to the
portal cavern.

Soldiers were guarding it, the new watch having taken
over from the previous night's guards. Four elves were
with them, and they let us pass, the elves looking more
than frightened.

"Stay back from the portal," I said, motioning for
everyone in the room to get away from it.

Even Minsheng hung back, giving Sen, Roth, Zephyr,
and me space to connect and work out what was going on.
After taking a couple of deep breaths to steady myself, I

reached out and tried to feel what was happening at the portal.

I blinked in surprise when it didn't feel the same as it had the night before. There was someone on the other side of the portal as before, but this was a different person, their control on the portal entirely different.

I reached out to feel who or what it might be. The elements they controlled seemed to be leaking through the portal. I reached farther to see if my control could go through what should have been a closed portal.

The portal resisted, but then the presence seemed to grow aware of me, connecting to me as I did to it. A woman's face filled my mind, and I gasped.

There was someone on the other side, but this wasn't the person I'd connected with the first time. This elf was as shocked as I was, but warm delight followed when she realized someone was here.

I laughed at the joy that came my way, nothing being offered or taken but emotion. Not sure what else to do, I pushed warmth her way and tried to show her I was a friend.

There was a moment where I thought she might disappear, but then I felt a similar emotion come back at me. It slowly faded, however, and the connection with it, her presence and control slipping until there was nothing there but the dormant static portal.

I couldn't move.

Did you all feel that too? I asked my mythicals.

Yes, Zephyr replied. *It was another elf on the other side of the portal.*

How?

I have no idea, but it confirms one thing. They're there.

After taking a few more deep breaths, I looked at Minsheng. My Shishou was staring at me, waiting for me to respond. Somehow my mouth found the words to tell him what I'd felt and what had happened, my mind still trying to catch up and process.

Minsheng came closer as I spoke, seeming to realize that whatever had happened wasn't happening anymore and it was safe for him to do so.

I found somewhere to sit down, many emotions and thoughts swirling in my head. Someone who had seemed friendly was on the other side of the portals, which made the experience of the night before more sinister. Who had been there the other time?

While I had no idea what was happening, I was scared. I had a feeling no one knew anything about it. At least, no one on this side of the portals.

And it was dangerous.

I ushered everyone away. I wanted to sit with my mythicals and Minsheng and discuss it, so I tried not to show my fear. I had no idea what to do now. I had been planning to make sure everyone was settled here and then go back to the warehouse for some much-needed rest and to train the elves there.

Instead, I wondered if I should stay, more worried than I had been. The second elf I had connected with didn't concern me much, but the first... He had felt very different.

Minsheng and I returned to the mess hall, which was empty. I was going to have to tell the President or whoever was in charge here as soon as I got my head around what was happening.

I wanted to find out a lot more, but for now, I wanted opinions from levelheaded mythicals I trusted.

"That was different, wasn't it?" Minsheng asked.

"Yes, a different elf was there, and we connected across the portal. It's as if it's not fully closed, but it takes great skill and power to breach the divide," I said, realizing how drained I was.

"And there are multiple elves on the other side, monitoring the portal." Minsheng continued my thought, taking it a step farther.

"Do you think that's what's happening when you get those readings? Elves are trying to reach through to see if anyone is here?" I asked.

"It's possible. Part of me hopes something like that is happening, but..." Minsheng's voice trailed off, and I knew he was thinking about the night before.

It wasn't easy to know what to do or where this was going. I could only keep trying to find more information and work out who or what was on the other side. But staying here longer also meant I wasn't able to go to the sea with Roth.

I will survive. It won't harm me not to be near or in the sea. I prefer it and miss it. You lead a far stranger life than I was expecting, but it is still an honor to be bonded with you. Roth's voice was warm and rich, and I felt all the emotions he did as he spoke.

I sent affection toward him; this wasn't easy on any of us. At the same time, Zephyr leaned closer. We had only one option before us: to stay at the portal and try to find out who or what was on the other side and if they were a threat to us. And we needed to make sure the right people knew what we were finding out.

"Give all this information to the folks here. I'm going to train until the next window you mentioned. Then we'll see who shows up and what happens."

"They'll want us to be careful," Minsheng said, getting to his feet.

"And we will. But if we can contact elves on the other side of the portal, I think we need to."

Minsheng nodded, thankfully not disagreeing.

It was a plan.

Not sure where to go to train where there was enough space, we went outside, inviting the off-duty elves who were awake to join us. I hurled the elements around for a while and Zephyr flew while Roth and Sen ran about and played.

As I created a twister, the dust beginning to swirl, I noticed I was drawing the attention of the soldiers around me. I concentrated, not wanting it to get out of control and hurt anyone, but I'd done it many times now.

Out in the heat of the Texas day, it was easier than it had ever been, my mind able to pull in the air and separate it before sending it spiraling. As it gained speed, it picked up dust until it felt like more dirt and sand than air.

I turned it faster still, moving it around the yard as I pleased.

It was only as I was bringing it back to the center of the area that I noticed the soldiers were watching what I was up to. I considered stopping and chilling the air back out, but I was enjoying having a fresh audience.

While I kept the twister spinning, I moved the earth, rippling it outward in waves and making statues of my mythicals for amusement. Finally, I reached for the water in the air and made it rain on a patch of earth in the back corner of the space.

I reached for the nearby plants and grew them to insane heights, forming them into whatever shapes I thought would look most interesting and hold up.

Finally, I was exhausted, and I let everything else go so I could safely wind down the twister and make sure it didn't hurt anyone. The dust fell with it, changing the layout of the land as it did. I finally tried to move it back to where it had been, which was easier said than done.

As I was doing the last part, all the soldiers who had come out to watch clapped and cheered.

You should take a bow or something, Zephyr said. I thought he was serious, but I looked his way and noticed he wasn't smiling.

I lifted an eyebrow.

What?

It's... Nothing.

It doesn't sound like nothing.

I miss when things were simple and we flew everywhere. But it's not your fault it's all changed.

Do you want to fly? I asked as I powered into the air. He flew lower as I did, the edges of his mouth curling up.

I joined with him in the air, and I could sense the relief in him. Before I could suggest a direction and tell Roth and Sen we'd be back soon, I was flying off to the horizon.

The wind blasted at me, blowing all of the tension away and my stress with it. Zephyr flew up, climbing fast as I focused on holding on and bringing in air to help keep me on his back.

It was exhilarating, but I didn't feel like we could do it for long. Sensing my unease at being too far from the others, Zephyr circled back and soared lower, tilting from one side to the other before diving.

Showing off as I had been, Zephyr attracted attention as well. He flew back and forth, demonstrating his skills and making it harder for me to stay with him.

When he banked again, I powered upward. It felt strange despite the practice I'd had. I preferred to ride Zephyr if I could, but he wanted to show the soldiers what he was capable of, and that was easier when I wasn't on his back.

We coordinated loops, rolls, and me falling and Zephyr catching me until I was dizzy and sick from the fast-paced turns and changes in direction. When I was tired and struggling to control enough air to stay in the sky, Zephyr came toward me, and we joined again.

Coming in slowly and gracefully, Zephyr landed. There was another round of cheering and clapping, and I could feel the smug delight radiating off the dragon beneath me.

I slid off his back, noticing Minsheng had appeared as well.

"Almost time," he stated as I walked closer.

I regretted showing off so much. How was I going to connect to the portal when I'd spent so much of my energy doing fancy tricks to amuse bored military personnel?

"We're going to need some lunch," I said as I walked past him, trying to sound like it wasn't as big a deal as it was.

Zephyr, if this doesn't work, I'm blaming you.

It's not my fault you spent ages making twisters.

I said I was blaming you, not that it was your fault.

Behind me, I heard Zephyr chuckle. Minsheng raised an eyebrow, but I didn't explain. Important things were about to happen, and I needed to eat if I was going to stand a chance of not screwing it up or missing my opportunity to connect to someone.

If Minsheng picked up on my behavior, he didn't say anything, just let me eat.

I was halfway through stuffing my face with a donut when his meter showed the portal was no longer dormant. Gulping down my half-chewed mouthful, I hurried to the portal chamber, feeling rather than seeing that Zephyr, Sen, and Roth were following.

As soon as I was in the room, I could feel the energy in the air. Someone was trying to reach through.

Without hesitation, I reached out, pushing through the force field the pillars created toward the dormant portal. It made my head hurt since I was more drained than I'd thought.

It didn't seem to matter. The moment I got close to the portal, something latched onto me.

Unable to breathe, I could feel it trying to pull me in closer and explore. This wasn't the delighted elf I'd connected with earlier. This was the same painful invasion as the first time.

Disconnect from it, Zephyr yelled.

Trying!

Try harder.

Not helping.

I concentrated, the pain growing as whoever connected with us tried to push through to my mythicals. It felt as if our bonds were being coated in a thick black substance that made them hard to sense.

Nothing seemed to break it off no matter how many times I tried to pull back and let go. It gripped me, and whoever was on the other side was sucking the energy out of me.

This isn't working, I sent to Zephyr, my panic rising. He felt far away as if he weren't standing right beside me.

Shitsticks.

This is worse than shitsticks.

Fucksticks?

Yeah, that.

Attack back if you can't defend us, Zephyr said, his voice sounding like it was coming through a crackly old phone line.

I winced, trying to find something inside me to push back with. Showing off earlier had been a bad idea. I had to hope I had the strength now.

As if I were fighting to take control of an element, I pushed forward and deeper into the portal. It hurt, the resistance stronger than normal, but I gritted my teeth, closed my eyes, and focused on going deeper.

Suddenly something gave way, the elements marked in a way I'd never experienced before and almost lifeless. I felt anger in waves as I tried to push all the elements back.

It was one of the hardest things I'd ever attempted to do, but it worked, the connection between me and it dropping away. Before it did, I caught an image of an elf in flowing black robes, his hands high and an aggressive smile on his face.

I pulled back through the portal and stepped away, my

body moving as my mind retreated. My head pounded and my body shook, so weak I wasn't sure I could stand much longer.

Worse than that, I could barely feel my bonds with Zephyr and the others. I worried that they'd been damaged.

"Make sure no one comes in here when the portal is active from now on," I said to whoever was nearest, not really seeing them as I stumbled toward my mythicals.

Sen bounded into my arms as I slumped toward Roth, and Zephyr leaned down so I was resting between him and the pegasus.

I didn't move, grateful they were still there and I could still feel them.

Sorry, I said to all three, not sure how else to express the guilt and fear mixed with gratitude and relief that whatever had happened was over.

I was still not sure what had happened, but I was glad it was over.

CHAPTER TEN

Once again, Sen, Zephyr, Roth, and I were watching the sunrise, but this time, it wasn't the sun over Texas. We were sitting on top of the warehouse in LA, back here after the craziness at the portal. We'd felt awful for almost twenty-four hours, as if our bond had been stretched. I'd barely been able to move while whoever it was connected to me.

When I had felt well enough to travel, the military had given us a ride to LA. We had been resting here for three days since then.

It had taken a long time for the bond to return to normal. That had been the worst part. Before, when I'd run down my powers and been disconnected from my bonds, they'd popped back as soon as I'd rested and recovered, and they'd been as strong as ever.

Whatever had happened to us, the damage was more severe. I'd worried that the bonds between us wouldn't come back, but they finally had, and we were a lot happier for it.

I'd been foolish, and I hadn't been able to stop apologizing for what it had almost cost us. I'd known something was lurking on the other side of the portals and that it might not be anything we wanted to tangle with, and I'd decided to show off to the soldiers instead of keeping my focus on why we were there.

I'd told the three mythicals beside me how sorry I was a thousand times, but I still felt guilty. With everything we were facing, I couldn't afford to make mistakes like that.

On top of that, I'd lost us time.

Somewhere out in the world, Cherisse was training elves to open a portal. They were getting stronger while I'd been hiding and licking my wounds. Minsheng had tried to keep things orderly at the Texas portal site.

I was very used to having him there to guide and train me. Having him somewhere different and focusing on another element of our world was strange. It had left me feeling more vulnerable as if I didn't know what I was doing anymore.

Today was the first day I felt as if we could change all that, however. Our bonds had returned, and we were fine. Despite our proximity to the sea, we'd not dared to venture out of the warehouse. We'd not have been able to handle a battle, but today, I felt well enough.

With the sun shining on us and the view across the city, we ate breakfast, other mythicals in the building joining us. It wasn't the huge communal meal we sometimes ate, but in the sun and after feeling so worried for so many days, it was everything we needed it to be.

There were more elves in the warehouse these days. Emily had kept them in order while we were gone.

I was once more grateful that I'd rescued her from the compound Jacobs had been holding her in. We'd probably saved her life, but she'd returned the favor at least once, and I was grateful for everything she was doing at the warehouse.

We were about to leave for the beach to do some training when a car pulled up outside that I recognized—my adoptive parents. They'd phoned to point out they'd not seen me for a long time, and it had only added to my guilt.

Although I still didn't get along with them as well as a child might with the people who raised her, they'd been very supportive since learning they'd been the parents of the world's most powerful elf.

I hurried downstairs. They hadn't yet met Roth, and I was eager to put a happy face on everything that was going on so they'd think their daughter was on top of the world. I hadn't told them about the trouble with the elves, although I'd had to tell them I'd been into Mexico since the news had reported on my trip back across the border.

After hugging them, I took a step back and introduced Roth. Mom's eyes went wide as she took in the stunning flying horse. His body was beautiful in the morning sunlight, and he bowed his head to my parents.

"It's an honor," he said, his voice halting and strange as he spoke. It wasn't easy for him to talk the way humans did, but it still made my mom beam more.

Zephyr came closer as well, greeting my dad with a dip of his head.

"Do I smell that beef jerky I mentioned I liked?" Zephyr asked.

With a grin, my dad pulled a big bag from behind his back. The smile on the dragon's scale-covered face grew bigger as I laughed. My parents were warming to having mythicals in their lives.

"What brought you to LA?" I asked, surprised they'd come all this way and unable to contain my curiosity any longer. They didn't live in the state, which meant they'd either arrived the night before and stayed somewhere, or they'd gotten up early to come see me.

They looked at each other as if they were trying to decide what to say and who should say it.

"When it came out that you weren't human, your dad and I had a good long chat about how little you knew about who you were. And we've seen you grow into something we're so proud of despite all the challenges," Mom said, her eyes watering as she did.

I couldn't respond, shocked by the depth of feeling in her voice. I had little experience with my parents being proud of me.

"Your mother and I wanted to see if we could help you learn more about who you are. Because it's clear your true parents must have been phenomenal."

As Dad spoke, he pulled an envelope out of his jacket.

"It took us some time to get a private investigator who would take the case. Your birth records are sealed, and there was a lot of resistance to us digging. But this guy managed to find out some stuff about who your parents might be."

I took the envelope with shaking hands, my mouth open and no words coming out.

"Don't open it now. There's not a lot there, and it's not

clear what it all means," Mom said. "I'm not sure there are any big answers, but given what you know and the people you have contact with, you might be able to take it further. Assuming you want to."

Still unable to speak and feeling as if they'd given me the most amazing gift since I'd found Zephyr's egg and changed the course of my life forever, I hugged them both. That they'd tried to find out what they could and probably paid an astronomical amount of money to do so made it all the more special.

Although I wanted to stay and talk to them for ages and look at the contents of the envelope I carried, Emily appeared. She came down ahead of the elves I was going to be training.

They paused when they saw us standing in the hallway, aware they'd interrupted, but I waved them forward.

"These are some of my elven friends," I said before introducing them all.

"We'll head to the beach and get started on training," Emily said before anyone could strike up a conversation.

Grateful that she'd picked up on the emotional moment, I nodded.

"If you need to go train or...whatever it is you do with those powers of yours, we can find something to see or do. Maybe we can all have dinner later?" Mom asked, her eyes full of hope.

"I would love that," I replied.

"Why don't you come to the beach as well and watch Aella in action?" Zephyr said before they could leave.

I lifted my eyebrows, surprised he'd said that. Although I'd always wanted to show them what I was capable of, it had been too dangerous, and I'd been so busy that going to see them wasn't easy.

But they were here, and it was clear from their faces that they loved the idea of coming with us to the beach.

Thanks, I said to Zephyr, knowing he'd picked up on a desire I'd never spoken and voiced it for me.

"Shall we meet you at the beach, then? Any particular area?" Dad asked as he pulled out his car keys and made for the door.

"No need," I said. "We can all fly if you want."

It was their turn to look shocked, but Roth stepped forward and offered to bear Mom. Zephyr grinned at my dad. My parents needed no further persuading. Instead of heading out the front, we climbed to the roof, and I helped Mom onto Roth's back.

Sen jumped onto my shoulder and tucked herself into my jacket, then as a group, we rose into the air. Dad whooped with delight as Zephyr swooped over the city, rising on the wind. At first, I worried about Mom and Roth as she clung to the winged horse's back and neck, but he flew smoothly, and she soon relaxed.

I powered upward with the air, controlling it and using it to give me lift and glide as I followed. For a moment, my world was perfect. My mythicals and I were in our element, enjoying flying together and taking others along for the ride.

It didn't take us long to get to the beach and land, and Mom thanked us. I tried to hide it, but I felt a flush of pride that something so simple could please people I cared about.

Emily and the others arrived before I could do much other than suggest that Mom and Dad wouldn't want to be too close to where we'd train but assured them they'd still be safe enough.

The elves all tumbled out, the smiles and delight on their faces making it obvious they'd been missing training with me as much as I'd needed it.

I encouraged everyone into groups, and we began. At first, I took control of the air, water, and sand beneath us, moving it around and shifting it gently so they could tell what I was controlling by sight. Then, as one, they attacked me, some fighting for control of the elements in my grasp.

Others hurled different forces at me. Zephyr, Roth, and Sen also trained. The dragon took the brunt of an air blast that would have knocked me off my feet. Roth caught a water blast, the liquid merging with his body and revitalizing him before it fell to the sand. Sen jumped and ran so fast she could dodge everything.

I saw the worried look on my mom's face and she put a hand over her mouth, but I was fresh and ready to push the elves. I lifted off the ground so no tremors could knock me off my feet, controlling the air around me to push myself up. It sent sand flying, but with so many elves trying to control it, it didn't get farther out than our group.

I was hit with a blast of air before Zephyr rose beside me and blocked it. I wobbled to one side but braced myself with another blast of air before someone took the control out of my grasp.

No sooner had I begun falling than Roth was there and caught me. The pegasus had regained some of his vitality from being near the sea and in the water, and he bore me high into the sky as I refocused my control.

When I was confident again, I launched off him and

rejoined the others, pushing them back and giving them a taste of their own medicine. Two of the water elves, along with Emily, chose that moment to make a tidal wave and have it come roaring up the beach. It was only about ten feet wide, but it was tall.

My dad gasped, but Roth and Zephyr came together in front of me, facing it so it wouldn't wash Sen and me away. The myconid leaped onto my shoulder as I focused on taking control.

Just before it hit the larger mythicals, I managed to steal control and broke it apart, sending it in all directions. It still soaked Roth and Zephyr, but my actions kept it from overwhelming them and us.

Once more, I was hit from behind by a blast of air. Sen squealed and almost fell out of my jacket as I tumbled forward. Right before I hit the sand, I managed to recover and lift us upright again.

Glancing at my parents again, I could see the fear on their faces, but they seemed to be proud of me. They had a delighted light in their eyes. It filled me with warmth and happiness and made me determined to keep going no matter what the elves I was training with threw at me.

Normally with so many more of them than me, they overwhelmed me, forcing me to yield before one of them accidentally hurt me. But could I achieve something else today? Could I push myself and see if some of them gave up instead?

I don't think it's wise, Zephyr said. *Cherisse knows we train here.*

It was a good point, and I knew I should listen to it, but

part of me didn't want to. We spent much of our time scared of what might happen next, and we'd only come back out into the world after three days of hiding and recuperating.

Despite my desire to push myself, however, I trained so hard I was in danger again. That meant I had to decide when to declare our tussle done.

While I was distracted, the air around me was once again snatched away, and I hit the sand before I could regain it. Still controlling the sand under me, I managed to cushion the fall and stop it from hurting Sen, but as I got up again, I knew I'd pushed myself hard.

I wanted to think of a final attack, a move that would give me the upper hand, but Emily chose that moment to hit with more water. It took all my concentration to stay upright before Roth dove between me and the spray and stole the brunt of its power.

Rocking, I did the only thing I could think to do and grabbed control of all the air I could, then powered up and out of reach of the other air elves.

Zephyr and Roth launched and followed, coming to my sides and holding there. I grinned, knowing the other elves couldn't reach me. They took that as the sign that our training session was done.

All of them stood down, letting the elements calm as I lowered myself. Zephyr, Roth, and I landed together and my parents got to their feet, clapping and smiling.

I grinned and nodded at the elves as they stood there looking pleased with themselves. All in all, it had been a good training session. The elves had been practicing, and what little I'd told them of the struggles with Cherisse and whoever was on the other side of the portal had been enough to make them train hard.

With plenty of us, we could do all sorts of things. We'd made progress, and I was back to full strength. I also had three powerful mythicals I could count on. Today was a good day.

CHAPTER ELEVEN

Another week had passed as we trained, growing stronger and teaching the elves around us how to take control and keep it. It had made me tougher too, going to bed each evening shattered and rising to eat and train some more.

My mom and dad had ended up sticking around for a couple of days, especially since the envelope they'd provided had given me more questions than answers. It appeared there was camera footage of the person who had left me as a baby.

That person had been found, but they lived in the middle of nowhere in Canada and didn't appear to have any ties with any elves. I couldn't tell if they were anything but human, which begged the question, "What did they have to do with it?"

We should go and visit them, Zephyr said over breakfast, snapping me out of worrying about it for the hundredth time.

Now? I asked.

Or tomorrow. We need to plan for it.

I thought about saying no, but he had a point. Was anything stopping us from going to find out? We'd been training hard, and there were questions still to be answered about the portals, but maybe something about my birth and parents could help me work out why I could control three elements when others couldn't.

Something beyond having all the great elves as ancestors.

I planned what we'd need to pack and how long it might take. The envelope we had contained a picture of the man we were looking for—a still. But as my adoptive parents had said, it had a lot more questions for us. I didn't look like him, and he didn't seem to have any contact with anyone.

Minsheng had been back for the last few days and had checked the name against the organization's database for me. There wasn't a match. On top of that, Emily's mother, Agent Crawley, had tried to help me find out more about him. Her information had been more confusing. He wasn't registered as being alive anymore.

But he was. The second picture of him in the envelope put him in Canada three days before Mom and Dad had given it to me. Whoever this was, he wanted people to think he was dead.

I had a lot of questions.

Before all the elves could get up and eat breakfast, my phone rang. The number was familiar but momentarily escaped my memory. After sighing loudly at being disturbed while eating, I answered.

"Aella, I know it's a long way to come, but I think we

need you at the site again," the President said, not introducing himself.

I lifted my eyebrows, hoping he was going to elaborate, but I received no explanation. What was going on?

"If I send an aircraft to get you from the nearest airport, something big enough for Zephyr, can you come straight here?"

This time there was a clear urgency in his voice, so I gave him an affirmative and jotted down the details of where we needed to go. He asked us to be there in half an hour, which would not be easy, but this was the President of the United States, and you didn't ignore a powerful person like that. Especially when he sounded like he was about to tear his hair out.

Within ten minutes, I had a bag packed, and once more, Minsheng insisted on coming with us. Thankfully, this time we didn't have to fly there and bring Minsheng with us. On top of that, we were rested, something we hadn't been the previous time. It wasn't ideal, but it was better.

I was also getting used to being summoned where needed and having my group travel together. It was as if we'd graduated from being a small fighting team to a group of mythicals who trained and helped others—consultants and experts in our field. It was weird, but it was also awesome.

We were soon in the air again, Minsheng on Zephyr once more, making me envious. I missed riding the dragon I loved. There was nothing as exhilarating as flying on the powerful mythical high above the ground and knowing it was where you'd been born to be.

It didn't take us long to get to the airfield where we

were being picked up. A massive cargo plane was sitting on the runway with the engine on, and several soldiers were waiting with it.

We landed right behind it and wasted no time going inside. There was a lot more space than a normal aircraft, but Zephyr still had to keep his wings tucked to his sides to fit through the back. I checked that he was okay before following him into the space. Part of me wanted to stay outside and ride in the free air, but half the reason they had sent it for us was to save my abilities.

In the end, I sat on the floor of the cargo hold beside Zephyr, leaning into him and resting. Roth laid down close to us, waves of concern and apprehension coming off him. Sen scampered about the plane, checking everything out with an excitement that amused the soldiers.

I sent comfort to Roth, letting him know that planes were nothing to fear, just humanity's way of flying.

This calmed him and allowed me to feel more relaxed as well, since the mythicals' emotions stopped me from feeling at ease if they were troubled. The bonds between us grew as our power increased. It was intense at times, but sitting in the plane, resting with them, I wouldn't change it.

Minsheng buried his head in a book, another tome with cracked leather bindings that looked like it might fall apart if anyone got too close to it. I wondered what was in it enough to watch him read it but not enough to ask. If there was anything useful within the yellowed pages, he'd tell me.

Rest, Zephyr said. *You've not been sleeping well since your parents gave you that information.*

I know, and it will be longer before we can try to find the guy.

We'll go when the time is right.

Zephyr's deep voice soothed me, the calm, powerful presence of the dragon one of my favorite things in the whole world. It was enough to make me relax, so I dozed off, leaning my head on his side with his tail around me.

When I woke up, the plane was coming in to land. Roth had come closer, his head also resting on Zephyr's tail. I noticed that a couple of the soldiers were looking our way, amused grins on their faces. It made me wonder what they thought of us, but I didn't get a chance to ask since the plane shook and rumbled.

"Turbulence?" I asked aloud, not having expected any when I could see the ground below us coming up fast.

"No. Something is hitting the plane," a soldier said as he rushed back. "Can you fly out of a moving plane?"

I nodded, not sure I could but willing to try. It couldn't be much harder than flying off the back of a moving dragon, could it?

With my affirmative, the soldier came up to me and led me to the back. Roth and Sen followed, but there was no way Zephyr could. There wasn't enough space for him to turn, and I was pretty sure he'd knock everyone else out of the plane or squash them if he tried.

Stay on the plane and protect Minsheng if he needs it, I said to Zephyr.

I thought the large mythical might object and try to get out of the plane anyway, but he nodded and looked at my Shishou. The part-dwarf's concern for himself and me was not helped by the soldier asking him to put on a parachute.

I got a glimpse of Minsheng doing so before the back opened and I was sucked toward the space. The soldier grabbed me and made sure I didn't fall out as Sen leaped into my arms and snuggled into my jacket.

I thought the gesture was sweet, but I wasn't scared of falling out of the plane. I'd fallen through the air so many times that another one gave me no qualms. Air was my domain, my dominant element, and the one I still felt the most at home with.

Before I could step forward again, a blast of air hit us, knocking us back. It felt forced, pushed by another elf. I snatched it, took control, and used the swirling air to keep the soldier and me on our feet.

Without another thought, I launched myself out of the plane, diving so I didn't get hit by the aircraft as it continued flying. I recognized the control of the air I'd been hit with but couldn't place it since the force was out of reach before I could be sure.

Slowing myself down and then turning, I powered after the plane. Roth leaped clear and began to fly. I was grateful for the backup, but I worried about him when it came to combat. He was stronger now, but he was neither too small to stay out of trouble like Sen nor big enough to protect both of us like Zephyr.

Roth flew closer to me, also turning to follow the plane, although he didn't manage to circle as quickly as I could and was soon struggling to keep up.

The plane wasn't going as fast as it could, but it wasn't slow either. That had been part of the point in it picking us up. It was supposed to make it quicker and easier to get to the base.

I couldn't see any elves attacking from anywhere, however. And how had they worked out where we were?

Until a couple of hours ago, we'd been in LA, and no one but the President and the soldiers had known we were coming.

Someone tried to take control of the air around me, and I had to concentrate. I felt the familiar elven mind again and fought hard to stay connected to the air holding me up. I darted to one side and then the other to make it harder to hit me.

Still not sure where they were, I reached out to the control of the elf, hoping they were in the sky like I was. With us moving so fast, the plane slowly inching farther ahead, I struggled to find them.

In the end, I opted to fly lower, knowing they couldn't be far away since my range was much greater than most air elves'. It wasn't going to be easy to find someone out here, but I had to try. They could clearly see me.

The plane continued to descend, and I spotted the portal site up ahead, the open space to one side of the main building appearing to be where the plane intended to set down. I headed that way, aware that Roth was falling behind, but whoever was attacking could easily target the plane, and Zephyr and Minsheng were aboard.

Feeling torn and wishing Roth could fly faster, I used some of my power to give him more lift and speed. It wasn't something he was used to me doing for him, but it let him keep up, and it took another worry from my mind.

It was only as the plane lowered more and I was hit again with a bolt of air that I finally pinpointed the culprit. Sitting on top of the plane were two air elves, both of them from Cherisse's cult.

Growling, I stole control of the air near them and

hurled it at them. They were ready for me and took control of more air to both throw my way and steady themselves.

I wasn't worried about the blasts coming at me. They weren't close enough to do much. I was far more concerned about what they'd do with the plane as it tried to land.

I'll let the soldiers know we have company, Zephyr said, helping me work toward a possible solution.

Let them know I'll try to solve the problem, but the landing could be bumpy, I replied as I pushed myself to fly closer. It wasn't going to be easy to distract two of them from this far away, but I had to do my best. They could kill people if they attacked the wrong part of the plane.

Aware I was leaving Roth behind and not sure what else to do for him, I moved my body into the most aerodynamic position I could think of and pushed myself hard, using more air to create a slipstream. It hurt, my body flying faster than I'd ever flown before as I caught up to the plane.

I locked eyes with the elves and blasted more air at them with all my control and focus. They stood their ground, however, using the air around them to keep themselves on the plane.

It gave me more time to get closer. I moved far faster than the slowing plane as I tried to hit them again. At the same time, I slowed down a little to keep them a certain distance away.

They slid to one side and I hit them yet again, wanting to get them off the plane once and for all. I felt them trying to take control away from me again, but I managed to keep hold of the air and fight their control. I blasted them one last time before they could recover, and they fell off the side of the plane.

I didn't want them to die, so I dove after them to follow their fall—and to make sure they didn't fly right back and hit the plane again. They soon recovered, making it clear they had plenty more power in the tank. It made me thankful I had rested the whole way here and had everything left to throw at them.

We fought for control of the air as they powered up again and I descended, the plane off to one side. I didn't have time for this to take long, and I didn't want it to.

Letting myself fall, I threw everything I had at them and took control of the air around them at the same time. Again they fell, tumbling and spinning as if there were in a washing machine.

I didn't let up following them, holding back my attacks to take control of the air around myself again and give the two elves time to use up their power to slow and stop themselves.

We continued fighting each other, getting lower and lower until I spotted more of the cult on the ground, an earth elf I recognized and some others.

Hesitating in the air, out of reach, I moved to put myself between them and the plane. As I did, I noticed that Roth was a long way behind, still trying to catch up.

Part of me wanted to fly to him and help him, but the plane was coming in to land, and I had a feeling these elves were going to try to crash it. Given how many lives were on it, I had no choice but to continue flying and fighting.

The group of elves turned my way, noticing the plane as well and moving closer. It was enough confirmation of their intent that I landed, taking control of the ground as I did. When I'd stabilized myself and made sure I was holding on to the ground they had built the runway on, I focused on the elves.

Before they could take too many steps, I shook the ground under them and grew the plants nearby to trip them and make their path harder. It wasn't easy to slow their advance. The elves fought my control as they blasted me with air. They knocked me back a couple of times. I balanced myself before resuming the fight.

I blocked their path, making it clear I would not let them hurt those behind me. After several minutes of trying, during which none of them managed to fight off my power, they glanced at each other.

As if all in agreement, they backed up. I simply held my ground, waiting to see where they went and keeping control. They slowly left, however, making me grateful that I hadn't had to use my abilities much that day so I could save it all for this battle. I was exhausted and shaking. Constantly fighting for control of the elements was taxing.

Behind me, the plane landed, my mind able to feel it as it touched the tarmac. Zephyr was no longer so far away from me. As soon as the engine was winding down and the soldiers were coming out of the back, I let go and relaxed.

For now, everyone was safe. And I could go back to figuring out why I was here.

CHAPTER TWELVE

I went straight to Zephyr, checking that he was all right and letting him make a fuss over me and check I hadn't harmed myself. Roth landed beside me a few seconds later, clearly exhausted.

I reached for him with my mind, sending comforting emotions his way. This was still hard for him to adjust, and we had put him through a lot. Despite how exhausted I felt after battling hard and holding control under a barrage of other minds, he felt worse.

Sen went over to him to comfort him as well, and the soldiers followed. Someone who looked to be in charge came up to me.

"What on earth was that?" the soldier asked me, his vocal tone making it clear he expected me to explain everything.

"Elves," I replied, not sure I liked being talked to that way. "Pissed-off elves who want that portal open."

"I gathered that much," he said, his words short as he glared at me, his chest puffed out and his gaze locked on me. "But why were they hitting the plane, and how did they find out you were aboard? Can you sense each other or something, and the elves can find you no matter what I do?"

"No." I folded my arms across my chest, not liking the man's attitude. "I don't know how they worked out I was aboard or why they thought they could attack and beat us. I'm far more powerful than they are. But they wanted the plane down. Was there anything else on it besides us?"

"I won't be discussing that with you." The soldier went to move past me, clearly thinking we were done with the conversation, but if there was something else I needed to know about, there was no way I was letting this go.

I stepped into his path again and put my hand up.

"You *will* be discussing this with me. I'm the best line of defense you have if Cherisse's elves are aware you have something. I need to know what I'm risking my life for."

The soldier glared at me as if he wanted to say something offensive, but I didn't back down.

"So, are you risking your life or not?" he asked a moment later. "You're either strong enough to save the day, or you're a liability."

I growled, reaching for the air around us and making it swirl.

Careful, Aella. I want to teach this clown a thing or two as well, but you can't hurt anyone.

I want to prove a point.

Zephyr sighed, and I could hear the resignation in it. It almost made me stop, but one look at the irritating man in front of me had me swirling the air faster, a twister growing around us.

We were calm in the middle, but as it grew in strength and speed, the center narrowed.

"I'm more powerful than your small mind can imagine," I said, gritting my teeth. "But the elves you face are strong, and you need my help. The President has called me here to help, so what is going on?"

The soldier didn't reply, staring me down and holding his ground no matter how close the air swirled around us.

We played chicken as I swirled it faster and tighter.

Enough, Aella, Zephyr growled. *It's getting too large and pulling in too much debris. You've lost this one. Don't hurt them.*

I didn't want to listen to Zephyr, and for a moment I didn't, letting the twister keep swirling although I stopped feeding it. I thought it wasn't going to make any difference, but it slowed.

I locked my eyes on the soldier as if I hadn't stopped.

Kill it, Zephyr said. *Let me try to get through to him.*

Fighting not to grin, I reached out to take control of the twister and properly slow it down. Before I could, it moved, however, coming in far closer on one side and whipping against a stack of the crates and supplies the rest of the soldiers had brought off the plane before our argument started.

It pulled in several cases as I used the air in the funnel to keep the soldier and me from being sucked into the vortex. The cases went flying, hitting a building before I could stop them.

Slowly I seized control again, making sure no one else was hurt or put in danger, but it was clear from the wide-eyed soldier in front of me and the other soldiers standing nearby with their mouths agape and plenty of distance between us that I'd taken things too far.

I gulped, not sure what to say or do, and a moment later, the President appeared. He took in the scene and then me standing with a soldier beside me, both of us no doubt looking windswept, the twister still dying and dropping its debris. The crates finished the decor, spilling their contents all over the ground and leaving dents in the building's walls.

"Do I want to know what happened here?" the President asked.

"I lost my temper. It won't happen again," I replied, unable to look at him.

"Good, because I was looking forward to the drinks in one of those crates. They'd shipped them in specifically for me," he said as he came closer.

I finally looked at him. "I'll make sure it's replaced. Along with everything else I broke."

"That won't be necessary. Accidents happen. But come, Aella, Major Kent, and Zephyr, Sen, and Roth. We should have a good long chat about the base security."

There was no way I was going to ignore the President's way of politely diffusing the situation but also making it clear he wanted to know what had happened in more detail.

I stepped out of the soldier's way and waited for Zephyr, Roth, and Sen to come to me before I moved. I knew Roth was exhausted, but he lifted his head and walked to my side.

Although I was grateful they wanted to stand by me after my outburst, I knew I had pushed things too far. I wasn't beyond being a bully, but I couldn't intimidate everyone into agreeing with me or giving me what I wanted.

Over the years, I'd had so many people doubt me that I'd gotten into the mindset of not hiding my confidence. If I had to, I faked being dominant so I didn't appear weak, but that wasn't going to work here. Not when it was clear that the soldiers didn't want to get along with the elves and the elves had no idea how to get along with the soldiers.

The President led us into a small room off to one side of the boardroom but I noticed the larger room wasn't unoccupied. Many of the elves and soldiers from the base were in there. The elves were on one side of the room, wide-eyed and unsure of themselves, and the soldiers were on the other. It looked as if lunch had been served between them, but no one was eating yet.

Again guilt washed over me. It was obvious I was supposed to be heading into that room and diffusing whatever was happening here. Instead, I'd made things a lot worse.

As soon as we were in the makeshift office, the major shut the door and looked at the President and me, then put his hands behind his back and stood at parade rest.

I glanced at Zephyr, not sure what to say. I'd let him, Roth, and Sen down, as well as all the other elves on the site.

It's okay. We all make mistakes, and we all lose our temper sometimes. You feel guilty, and you realize it was wrong. So many would think they were right. I'll be at your side, but you need to say you're sorry.

And I need not to do it again.

117

Yes. And that.

Thank you for trying to stop me.

I'm always with you, good or bad.

I swallowed as the President cleared his throat.

"I understand that the two of you had a disagreement. Aella, I've seen what you're capable of before now. What else do I need to know?"

"It was my fault," I said without hesitation. "I lost my temper, and I shouldn't have. It won't be something I repeat."

"Well, I won't deny I appreciate the honesty. I know these things are never one-sided. Something made you angry enough to start a twister. I understand that's no easy feat for an air elf, even one as strong as you."

I blinked, having expected to be yelled at, admonished, or worse. Here was a man telling me he understood that despite me acting in a way I shouldn't, he was seeking to solve the problem.

"Miss Carter asked to know what else we'd brought on the plane. I informed her it wasn't information I could divulge. She—"

"Ah. Well, that is something that I can sort out. Aella is to be given all information she asks for. She is the final and best line of defense for this portal, and her understanding and knowledge are valuable enough not to keep her in the dark."

"Understood, sir," the soldier said, still not looking my way.

I paused, wanting to ask what I hadn't been told but pretty sure it wasn't the right time. Although I was curious and I knew there was something important, I needed to smooth this over and make sure the soldiers and the elves were getting along with each other.

"Right. Now, I believe this won't happen again, and I'm comfortable trusting both of you, but I want to be sure that you are all going to work together if I'm not here."

"I can handle that," I replied. The soldier didn't respond. He gulped as every eye turned to him.

"It seems you have something on your mind, Major. You might want to say it and be done. Unless it's something no sensible man would say, in which case you probably ought to tell me you can be respectful to Aella and the bonded creatures with her."

"It's..." The soldier looked at me. "They've received no training. They've pledged no allegiance. They're like hiring mercenaries, except we don't know they want money."

I laughed, unable to help it.

"You know I'm an American citizen, right?" I asked. "And partially human. I might not have enlisted in a military division, but I'm trained for battle, and there are many people in this country I wish to protect, human and elf alike. I'm an ally, and my motives match yours, I imagine. I want to use the skills I have to keep this nation and the world safe from those who would harm it."

This seemed to have an impact. The soldier nodded after studying me and relaxed a little.

"Even if I did only want to protect other elves? I don't want that portal open, and I don't want anyone else getting hurt. We're temporary allies if nothing else."

"I can work with that," he said finally. "But I'd appreciate not ever having to be inside one of your twisters again. They're terrifying, and I don't know how you managed to stay so calm."

"I can fly. It helps. Plus, I've faced bullets, rockets, bombs, elves who want me dead and are trying to make me fall out of the sky, and countless soldiers and military personnel. A twister I'm controlling isn't that scary anymore."

The major lifted his eyebrows as I spoke. I smiled to let him know it was only friendly banter. Dark humor about what I'd faced in the past.

"Right. If we're all friends again and happy to be on the same team, I need to ask a favor of you. There's a group of elves and soldiers next door who could use some help to find a similar team spirit, especially given what happened here last night."

"Should I be asking them what happened, or you?" I said as the President moved to the door.

"It's probably going to be more chaotic but have better long-term results if they tell you themselves," he replied, opening the door before any of us could say anything else.

I took a deep breath and waited for Zephyr, Sen, and Roth to join me before I moved toward the boardroom. Zephyr came close while Sen rested on Roth's back. I leaned into the dragon and his smooth scales.

Thank you, I thought, still feeling pretty small.

We'll get through this together, but you took a good first step. You owned up to your mistake right away. Let's hope we can help the others do something similar.

Feeling the warmth of Zephyr's emotions, I tried to calm down. I needed to keep a level head.

The elves and soldiers had filled plates with food and

started eating before we joined them. I didn't hesitate to do the same, hungry after draining my power.

This seemed to help the elves relax, and they dug in. I grabbed another plate and handed it to the major.

"I owe you a drink after this is all over," I said as he took it from me.

"Sounds like an idea I can get behind. Do you have any fancy elven drinks I might like to try?" he asked as I offered him some potato salad.

"You know, I have no idea." I looked at the other elves as I finished speaking, inviting one of them to tell us if there were.

At first, no one moved, then an elf from the Sanctuary I recognized as a fire elemental leaned forward and began describing something that sounded like mead.

The tension left the room as everyone began talking about and comparing their favorite drinks and cocktails, finding common ground. They got closer to the table and the food while they talked.

I was heading to the table for a third plateful when I caught the President's eye. He gave me an almost imperceptible nod; I'd managed to rescue the situation a little, but the hard work was still to come. One conversation about drinks wouldn't get us past whatever had happened, and I still had a lot of questions.

Especially about what had been on that plane.

CHAPTER THIRTEEN

Exhaling, I tried to calm the rapid beating of my heart. The silence that filled the boardroom was so thick that I could have heard one of Zephyr's scales fall off. The crunch moment had come and I'd dared to ask everyone what had happened over the last night.

No one had answered. Not one of them.

"I understand all of you were there, right?" I asked when no one spoke.

"There was my team and me," Seth said. He was the first to look me in the eye and get on with it.

My heart sank. As much as Seth had improved, he was still one of the hotheads among the elves. I wasn't sure I was going to like what he would say.

I suspected Cherisse's cult had attacked, much as they had during the day, and the elves had been needed to defend the portal, but what could have gone wrong?

Seth seemed to read my mind and explained how the attack had begun. No one interrupted him until he got to the part where the elves had once again breached the cavern.

"Two of the elves ran away," one of the soldiers said, the anger in his tone clear.

Several elves, including Seth, tried to talk, yelling their indignation. I lifted my hands and made the air shift around to get their attention, making sure nothing I did would hurt anyone.

They fell silent, but the atmosphere was icy again. If I'd been a fire elemental, I'd have set one blazing in some open space to make a joke and see if it helped.

Instead, I exhaled. Before I could say anything, Zephyr stepped forward.

"In my time with the elves, I've never known any of them to run away from trouble or the people who need them. It's not done. Your soldiers are trained to defend others and stick by their comrades, and so are elves."

"Zephyr speaks the truth," Seth said as he stood. "The elves with me wouldn't run, not when so much is at stake. They went to get other elves, knowing we needed backup and the soldiers were on the way."

I nodded, motioning for Seth to continue when everyone was calm and listening again.

He continued to describe the fight. I noticed that every time the soldiers went to interrupt, the major shook his head and made them wait. At first, Seth told me only what the elves had done, how they'd fought the elements and kept the attackers at bay. Then he told me about the soldiers' actions.

I couldn't immediately see where the problem lay. Seth's words and description showed the groups working together, the elves defending against the elements and doing their best to hold a line, while the soldiers used tranks to take out any elves who showed themselves.

I listened, sure there was more coming. There had to be, and it made me worry. Had the elves broken through?

Let them tell their story, Zephyr reminded me. *Whatever happened, they must have succeeded in the end, or we wouldn't be here.*

It was a good point, and once again, I was thankful for Zephyr and the calm he represented. I was panicking about something I didn't need to.

Finally, Seth got to where everything had gone wrong, but it wasn't in the way I expected. Instead of the elves having broken through to the portal and threatening to break the pillars to keep it from being opened again, someone had pushed them back.

While the attack had been happening, there had been something else. The portal had grown active, as it had when Minsheng had been monitoring it. Only this time, I wasn't the one there to receive the incoming call from whoever was on the other side. This time, something had shaken the entire area as if they sensed the presence of many elves.

I listened as Seth talked about the chaos as the barriers were sucked in and destroyed. An elf had been injured, as well as two soldiers who had less of an idea about what was going on than the elves. Seth had connected to whoever was on the other side without being sure he was okay with that.

The soldiers once again interjected, but this time they weren't full of anger at the elves, simply wishing to explain what it had looked like to them. Seth had appeared to stick right by the portal boundary, turning to it and looking as if he was going to attempt the very thing we didn't want.

Naturally, the soldiers had reacted, and the major had shot Seth with a dart.

I didn't need Seth to continue or anyone else to tell me it had knocked out Seth and chaos had ensued. The elves and the soldiers wouldn't have trusted each other after that, even if they were talking about it calmly now.

As some of them tried to explain who they had shot and why, or who they'd hit with what elements, I held up a hand again. This time I didn't use my abilities, but it was enough to get everyone to stop talking.

"It's clear there is much we don't understand about this portal and what lies on the other side, and we need to learn as much as we can," I said. "To make sure that we don't end up with a free-for-all like that again."

There were sheepish looks on the faces of soldiers and elves alike, but there was more work to do. We needed to become one team and feel like it. It should have been hard to shoot one of them down. It should be difficult to hurt each other, and it was partially my fault that it wasn't harder.

I looked around the group. Seeing lots of eager faces, I tried to work out what to do differently.

"It's clear that people shouldn't get too close to the portal. Even more so than before. And it's clear that shooting each other isn't a good idea."

There were some snickers at my last statement from elves and soldiers alike, and it made me grin. It seemed that

I had helped break the ice and put some of the tension to bed.

"For my part in it all, I am truly sorry," the major said. "I was more than liberal with the darts and didn't always take care where an elf was or how much danger they were in."

"I'm sorry as well. I should have tried to get away from whatever was on the other side of the portal. Aella had warned us about it, but I let my curiosity get the better of me." Seth exhaled as he sat back down again.

I stayed quiet as lots of the others apologized to each other. Then the room was silent, everyone having said what they needed to.

Nicely done, Zephyr said.

I'm pretty sure that was more you than me, but it also seemed to happen all on its own.

No. You got them to stop bickering at the beginning and asked the right questions. I told them what they knew: that everyone here is a soldier of one type or another. Someone willing to fight for what they believe is right.

Yes. We're all fighters.

And fighters sometimes challenge each other in their determination to make sure everyone is safe. You showed them they were on the same side.

I exhaled and smiled at the major, noting the grin on the President's face. It seemed he was pleased with how the meeting had gone.

Talk of dessert only added to the relaxed mood, and someone wheeled in a large cart full of cakes, cookies, and drinks. I had a feeling the President had been behind that too, but I wasn't complaining.

I made sure Sen and Roth were also okay. The winged

horse was still more subdued than normal.

It's hard being so far from the shore, he said as I went to his side. *And there is something here that doesn't feel right. It's hard to place. The atmosphere is...tainted.*

I exhaled, knowing Roth was right. I didn't doubt that there was something bad on the other side of the portal somewhere. Something we didn't want to let through. But it was trying to get to us.

Helping Roth eat and rest, I tried not to worry about it for now. We were doing all we could to stop anything bad from happening. It was all we could do. And take care of each other as much as possible.

When I was finishing my second helping of a large fruit pie, I heard the sound of running feet.

"Attack!" someone yelled from the corridor.

Everyone in the room responded when the door was flung open. Men in security uniforms flocked to the President, and the soldiers and elves rushed for the open door. I was one of many as I and my mythicals did the same, all of us ready to defend.

Grateful we'd been able to eat, I took control of the air around my body, pushing my limbs faster and weaving through the others to get to the portal room ahead of the majority.

I felt Zephyr and Sen running behind me, but Roth was slower, the tug on my stomach letting me know he was lagging. Once again, I had to ignore it as I powered into the main room of the compound.

At the far end of the area, I could see soldiers fighting several fires. I rushed forward, creating a box of air around one. It choked off the oxygen supply, but I could feel more happening as I ran around the edge of the portal, leading the charge.

Sen bounded onto my shoulder, still faster than me despite my magical boost. She hung onto me as I ran toward the other elves I could feel.

I wasn't far from the fires, and the one I'd boxed was beginning to die when I felt the creeping water of an elf trying to make its way in slowly from almost directly below me.

Stepping back and holding my arms out so no one else would make the mistake of stepping on top, I tried to pull the water away from the elf controlling it, only then recognizing the tell-tale signature of one particular water elf. Cherisse was here, and that was entirely unexpected.

I fought her control, trying to find a way to take the water away from her while calling for more water elves. The rest of the water elementals were too busy trying to suck water into the room to put the fires out.

The soldiers were all standing around, waiting with dart guns in their hands and making it clear they weren't sure what to do or how to go about defending against an enemy they couldn't see.

A few had fire extinguishers, but there were so many fires popping up and the canisters ran out so quickly that there was little the soldiers could do.

I focused on fighting as an elf broke through on the other side of the cavern. Zephyr came to my side, his head poised over the place Cherisse was trying to break through. I felt and heard him shift his body, preparing to exhale his gas weapon at the reckless elf who wanted to open portals and was willing to sacrifice others to do so.

A couple of times, I managed to get control from Cherisse, but she was quick to fight back and take the water into her control again. Although I never gave up, she crept closer, the water more than enough to erode the soil effectively.

Keeping an eye on the fight that was raging to my left, I pushed one last time. This time I heard a muffled yelp as if I'd shoved someone over. Part of me hoped it was Cherisse, but I knew her voice and how much she put on a display. Riding in her wake was another water elf. One of them must have done it.

No sooner had I thought this than the earth in front of me crumbled, threatening to tip me and my mythicals into the hole along with several soldiers. I reached for it with my mind, trying to toughen it up and block the route again, but someone was attacking my control.

"Need help over here," I called, hoping someone could respond.

There are far more elves than normal, Zephyr replied. *Hold them as best you can. There are more soldiers on the way.*

I exhaled, feeling Zephyr's panic and a similar emotion coming from Roth. I wanted to go to them, but I didn't get a chance. Cherisse appeared several feet below me, our eyes locking on each other.

With her were three other elves, wearing dark clothing and away from the rest of the elves. I was bombarded with elements, the air around me being challenged as the water Cherisse had been holding sprayed at me in a fine mist that made it hard to see.

I backed up a couple of steps, feeling with my mind for the air and snatching as much control as I could. At the same time, I tried once more to take control of the water, but it cost my control of the earth, and before more than a couple of seconds had passed, I was knocked off my feet.

I went flying back, trying to use the air to cushion Sen and me. It worked, but control was taken from me at the last moment, making me fall on my back anyway. The noises of elves clashing, fires burning, the earth shaking, and the soldiers firing dart after dart filled the air as I struggled back to my feet. Sen was on the ground near me, having tumbled off me as I fell.

Cherisse and the elves with her ignored me, instead focusing on the portal and the pillars. I got to my feet, scooping up Sen before a soldier could trample her, and surveyed the area. The portal room was full of people, elves fighting elves and soldiers doing their best to fire at only the elves who shouldn't have been there.

More than once, a dart made its way toward the wrong elf, and a defender slipped into an unconscious state.

This isn't working, I called to Zephyr as he stomped a large paw down on one fire and put it out. *We need to get the numbers down. It's as if they've brought the entire mountain with them.*

Guide the darts. Get the soldiers to shoot more and make sure they hit.

Exhale some gas as well, I replied since he'd considered it earlier.

Zephyr hesitated, then delivered the vapor I needed.

Letting go of all the other elements and drawing closer to Zephyr, I took control of as much of the air as I could as well as the gas cloud he'd given me. I moved the gas and helped direct the soldiers' darts, taking out more elves as they rushed into the cavern from the holes they'd broken through with.

It wasn't easy to direct the flow of so much at once with other air elves trying to stop me, but I focused on taking them out first, surprising soldiers as they fired at one target and the elf beside it was hit.

Slowly I turned the tide, more elves collapsing, sedated, or paralyzed than were pouring into the cavern. I also noticed fewer challenging me, allowing me to focus better.

Aella, Cherisse is trying to break a pillar, Zephyr shouted.

I switched my focus to her, furious that I'd let my guard down. I'd helped the others so much that I had neglected the most powerful elves in the room. All four of them were standing in the force field of the pillars, straining as they tried to keep each other alive and tackle the pillars.

I rushed closer, hoping the soldiers could handle the rest of the elves. Zephyr exhaled again, and I swept the gas over to the force field. It resisted that, but I pushed for control of the area, continuing to fight with only my air element.

After I enveloped the nearest elf in the cloud, she flopped. I used the air to pull her out of the field and blasted the other three as hard as I could to push them out of the field too.

They all fell back, Cherisse's eyes locked on me. If looks could kill, I'd have been dead, but I stood my ground and held onto my control of the air. Zephyr rose above me as Sen and Roth came running up.

"You're not opening this portal," I said. "Or any portal. Something evil lies on the other side."

Cherisse stepped closer before another of the elves with

her put a hand on her shoulder, his large form holding her in check. I took a step closer as well, feeling my mythicals do the same.

As she looked at the portal, which was safe from her for now, she frowned. She was calmer, but plenty was still happening in her mind.

"I think I understand this better than you do," Cherisse finally replied. "You want to be the all-powerful one. The one to open this. The one to protect this world from whatever you decide it needs to be protected from. You're no better than anyone else, but I won't let you stop me. *We* won't let you stop *us*."

Cherisse dodged as a dart came her way, ending her little speech.

"Retreat," she yelled, and the guy beside her picked up the elf I'd paralyzed with Zephyr's gas and stepped out of the forcefield.

Even faster than they had appeared, the elves hurried away. The soldiers tried to shoot more of them, but they moved fast and threw earth barriers with surprising speed and accuracy.

They were getting better at combating the soldiers, and they'd been training to fight other elves their whole lives.

I went to follow them, not sure what I wanted to do but terrified that a second attack from them would be too much. Zephyr's tail swept around me, however.

Let them go. You don't have the strength to take them on alone, and the elves here are exhausted. There are too many of them this time.

I frowned, but Zephyr was right. There *were* too many.

CHAPTER FOURTEEN

I couldn't speak. My body ached from being thrown around, dropped from the sky, and everything in between. It was a new day, but the previous one had left me overtaxed.

The moment I was awake, I thought about Cherisse and her attack on the portal. She was more powerful than I remembered, even if I had also grown. With so many more battle-ready elves, she clearly had the advantage.

Since we'd managed to make them flee, the elves on the base had either been resting so as to be ready to ward off another attack or working on securing the portal cavern further.

I'd been part of the latter team, putting my earth elemental powers to good use by reinforcing the rock and making it harder for the elves to tunnel into the cavern. I was pretty sure it wouldn't keep them out in the long term, but it would slow them down and drain them when next they attacked. With any luck, it would turn the tide in a battle.

Despite the preparations, I wasn't in a good mood. The attack had shown one thing very clearly. Cherisse had a powerful set of four elves, and they were willing to put themselves in a lot of danger to get a portal open. I had to stop them, but I was at a loss as to how.

They had a portal in their mountain, and it made me worry that if we defended this one well enough, eventually, she would open her own. I was also puzzled why she hadn't done so.

As my alarm went off for the fourth time, Zephyr nuzzled me with his head. He was in dragon form beside me. It was finally time to get up. Groaning as my stiff muscles protested, I finally got myself going.

We'll train and teach them as best we can, and then we might want to consider Gwaelon's offer, Zephyr said.

I was hoping we wouldn't have to ask someone to be in that much danger, I replied as I picked up Sen and popped her on my shoulder. Roth had finally gotten up, his face serious and his emotions darker than I'd have liked.

Trying to reassure the newest, most apprehensive mythical bonded to me, I moved to the door.

He volunteered to go become a spy. You can't think of it like that. We all want to play our part in some way, and we know he's reliable and trustworthy.

Do we? We would have said the same of Chris a year ago.

Good point. But Chris wasn't from the Sanctuary. Or offering to risk his life. Sure, he helped us loads, but he was never in harm's way.

I exhaled at Zephyr's words, knowing he was probably right. And either way, we couldn't worry about it yet. We had an elven training session to run and meetings to attend with soldiers and diplomatic figures alike.

But first, breakfast. No elemental elf started the day without the biggest breakfast they could get, and I certainly wouldn't.

To my surprise, the major had saved me and my mythicals a seat at one of the larger tables, and some of the foods I liked to eat were there.

"Thanks," I said as I sat and helped Sen get herself some water to stick her roots in and drink.

"I figured I owed you and the other elves here. Yesterday's fight was...eye-opening. If you hadn't helped us take out so many of them, we'd have been overrun. I had no idea you could be so controlled and destructive in so many ways."

"I've been training hard for years, like you. And I was kidnapped by Cherisse and her elves a few months back. That was harder. The elements in her mountain are marked. Makes it harder for me to control them and easier on her," I replied, not sure where the story and the vulnerability that went with it had come from.

The major lifted his eyebrows but didn't interrupt. Instead, he passed me more bacon and poured me some juice. I had to admit, I could get used to someone who anticipated my food-based desires so well.

I can do it better, Zephyr said, the mock jealousy that came with it almost making me snort my first mouthful of liquid. The major looked at me, surprised.

"Sorry. Zephyr can talk into my head, and he decided that was a good time for a joke. It wasn't at your expense, and he should definitely not do it again." I shot Zephyr a look as the major smiled and shook his head.

"That must be weird, but I can see why you all make such a great team. I'm glad you're on our side, Aella. And the rest of the men too."

"And I'm glad you're on my team this time around. I've fought more than enough soldiers to last a lifetime."

We fell into silence as we ate and then went to train. I had offered to do one more session with the elves and the soldiers on the base so they could see what we were capable of and work out ways to complement each other better.

After being called here to sort out issues with the elves and soldiers not cooperating, finding they were so excited to train together was a relief, even if I felt nervous about the number of folks I'd be training. Some of the elves had been at the Sanctuary and had trained alongside me in the past. I didn't feel qualified to teach them since the elven masters in the haven had far more experience with their elements, but someone had to train people here.

Seth was also going to help, keeping the fire elves pushing themselves so I didn't have to worry about that element. Part of me had hoped I'd have access to that element by now, but I was still learning how to use water and refining my use of earth. The only one I felt I had enough experience with was air.

Still, the elves lined up, ready to show the soldiers what they could do. I'd thought back through the lessons I'd received in the past teaching teamwork and skilled precision. Many of the elves in front of me had a reasonable level of power, and they'd volunteered for that reason, but few of them knew how to work in a group and with a level of control that enabled that to go smoothly. They had never needed to.

I split the groups of elementals into pairs, water with fire elves and earth with air elves, then had them face a matching elemental pair. I had the air and earth elementals sneak up on each other, using the earth and air to keep themselves from being detected. The water and fire elves were to work together to see who could keep their fire burning longest.

It wasn't a perfect way to begin, but it gave them ways to work with an elf of a different element—and it was going to look awesome.

Although I wanted to be training and practicing with them, I had a lot of the elves using their abilities, and someone had to stay rested and strong to defend the base. I watched, giving advice where I could to the elements I was responsible for.

They took a while to get into the challenge, but they eventually managed it, and the soldiers watched. As the advice I could give waned, I backed up, and the major came to stand beside me.

"This is impressive. This is something you can do as well?" the major asked a moment later.

"I can't control fire yet."

"Yet?"

"Yeah. No other elf can control more than one element well, but I can control three. Everyone assumes I will control all four at some point."

"That explains some of why you're so badass compared

to these elves. And so confident. You don't need a team most of the time."

"Oh, I have a team," I replied, looking at my mythicals. Roth was sitting in a tub of saltwater again, but Sen was running about the training grounds, helping and hindering as she saw fit. Zephyr was in the sky, keeping a lookout and stretching his wings.

I didn't like having him so far from me, but I didn't want to force him to stick to one place.

As if he sensed us watching, Zephyr dove, plummeting at an alarming rate. I grinned, pretty sure he was showing off but finding it funny.

The soldiers looked up as he flew by, pulling up at the last moment to skim above the base, his belly mere inches off the surface of the roof. The sun glinted off his scales, making him dazzlingly bright before he flapped several times, his large wings fully extended.

Each downbeat blasted air across the grounds, although I kept it from blasting across the elves as they trained; then he was high in the sky again. He rolled to one side and then the other, tucking his wings each time, only to spread them again. I'd seen him do that many times while flying over the beach in LA while I stood upon the sand.

But it was clear that others weren't used to it, and their mouths fell open as they stared.

A moment later, Zephyr landed beside me, so controlled he barely puffed up any dirt. He tucked his wings to his sides.

Nicely done, I said.

I hope so. Sometimes I want to show everyone what we're all capable of.

Oh, I'd rather they were focused on you instead of me a thousand times over. Feel free to draw attention to yourself.

Zephyr chuckled, but we both knew it wasn't true. Part of me was getting used to being a special elf who could do far more, and Zephyr appreciated not having everyone want to pet him, talk to him, or take a picture. It could be tiring.

As soon as I thought the elves had been trying for long enough, most of the elves having tested their opponents twice, I stepped forward and stopped them. Some of the fires were still burning, and a few of the successful elves had to be persuaded to uncover themselves, but eventually, I had them back in neat rows.

I think we're going to need more space, I said to Zephyr as I thought about the next bit. *And the soldiers are going to have to move farther back.*

With that, my three mythicals got to their feet and encouraged the human part of our audience to step back and the rest to spread out a little. As we'd practiced on previous occasions, I had elementals of the same type face each other and fight for control of the area around them.

That meant I had to create fire pits and hand out water buckets as well as seeds for plants, but the major and my mythicals helped.

As soon as I had them calmly waiting where I wanted them, I commanded them to begin. Last man standing. For a moment, nothing seemed to happen; no doubt all of them warring with their minds. Finally, the elements moved, earth shaking, plants growing, wind blasting elves off their feet, water filling the sky, and fires lighting everything up.

Although I knew it was a training exercise, the power

on display made me step back. These elves knew how to sling the elements around, and they weren't pulling their punches.

I reached out with my mind, fighting my natural urge to take control as I did, trying to feel what was going on before it happened. I used my abilities to catch something that went flying or keep the elements within the area and the watching soldiers safe.

There was nothing but awe on the soldier's faces; they looked as riveted as I was. They and I were worried this was going to get violent, but I was there to make sure no one was hit too hard with anything deadly.

After ten minutes, I called a halt. Most battles against other elves didn't last much longer than that, one getting the upper hand or running out of steam. I wanted them all to have something left.

"Take a break and have a snack," I said, hoping they had enough left in them.

I wanted to do one last thing with them. Grinning as if he anticipated what I was about to ask the group to do, Seth came up to me.

"I could do with your help," I said. "You and I are still very fresh, and we need a challenge."

"I thought you'd never ask," Seth replied, not one to shy away from showing off.

I laughed at the confident way he turned to stand on my other side. It was only then that I noticed the President had come out of his office to watch. He gave me a brief nod as he leaned against a wall in the shade.

Trying not to think about the extra pressure and wanting to impress the man, I stepped forward. As soon as the elves had finished their snacks, I called them back, asking them to mingle and not huddle in their elements.

"Who wants to see if they can beat Seth, me, and the mythicals?" I asked, raising my voice so everyone outside could hear me.

There was a chorus of cheers at the thought of it before all of them grew more serious, their eyes on Seth or me for the most part. Zephyr came close, and Roth got out of his bath. I couldn't see Sen among the elves, but I could feel her and noticed she was staying where she was as if she were up to something.

"Are you sure about this?" I asked Seth, and he nodded and grinned in response, pushing up his sleeves and looking at the elves in front of us.

"Now!" I yelled, giving no more warning.

The training ground exploded into life, more than fifty elves using the elements to attack us. I grabbed what I could and focused on my control. As I did, Roth ran at a jet of water, absorbing it harmlessly before it fell to the ground at his feet. A moment later, Zephyr blocked another water blast.

Seth and I glanced each other's way before we unleashed our power. I blasted the entire front row of elves, sending fire, water, air, and earth elementals alike scattering. A few air elves held up, their abilities allowing them to slow and recover with the air near them. I followed it with water, using it only on non-water elementals.

Finally I grabbed the plants the elves had grown in the previous fight and lashed out with them. It was an impressive combo, but it wasn't long before the elves were countering and hurling elements at me again. Once more, my mythicals defended me from two of them, Seth having to defend himself for the most part.

Just as I thought Seth might be overwhelmed, Roth got in the way of a water stream meant for me, but instead of making it fall to the ground, he redirected it, putting out a fire that had been forming near Seth.

The fire elf grinned as steam rose and water hissed in the heat. It was an impressive display of skill from my mythical, and it showed that Roth was getting the idea about how to help in battle with others.

With this bit of aid, however, the elves targeted both of us, water, earth, and air directed at Seth and me. Zephyr swooped down again, taking a blast that should have knocked us off our feet. Sen chose her moment.

A large plant-based ball came rolling toward us, Sen on top of it and propelling it with her feet. My eyes going wide as I stepped back alerted some of the elves to what was coming as it barreled into them and knocked them over like bowling pins.

She whooped in delight as I took control of it and helped her steer until she jumped down to avoid a blast of water Roth didn't stop in time. It was enough of a distraction, however, that Seth and I gained the upper hand. Someone set light to the large ball, forcing me to douse the flames so no one was burned by it, but the elves were giving up now.

Their powers spent, or exhausted enough they were unwilling to continue, elf after elf backed off, and Seth and I gained more and more control.

As suddenly as it had begun, the challenge was over.

Seth and I stood victorious beside each other. Zephyr landed behind me, and Sen and Roth walked closer. We'd won for the first time. I knew we'd started with an advantage, neither of us drained while they had been training, but we'd put up an epic display and worked together well.

The soldiers erupted in applause and started coming forward. At first, I was worried that the other elves would feel disheartened, but they had smiles on their faces as everyone got to their feet and came closer. Soldiers congratulated the elves, praising moves and generally being encouraging.

Feeling like I'd finally gotten something right, I made sure they knew they'd done well, calling everyone to me and praising them. I'd woken up worried that Cherisse would walk all over these elves if I wasn't here but had finished our training knowing that she wouldn't. These elves were determined and learning fast.

CHAPTER FIFTEEN

High in the sky on Zephyr's back, I relaxed when the Sanctuary came into view. It was a welcome sight and a safe place for all of us. I could feel the tiredness emanating from Roth. Sen was asleep in my jacket.

After training and talking to the President about the threat, we'd agreed that we needed more information. I'd risen into the sky with Zephyr and the others to head back to the Sanctuary. Although I didn't want to take Gwaelon up on his offer, it was looking like I had to.

Firstly, however, I was going to talk to the council. They had once frustrated me by not keeping me in the loop about important things, but I didn't intend to keep them in the dark about this.

Zephyr landed near the border, once again being polite and letting the Sanctuary follow its usual protocols for visitors. As far as I knew, we were the only regular visitors who flew in. They met everyone else at the perimeter.

As always, we requested to see the council and walked the rest of the way. It was nice to stretch my legs after several hours of flying. I would have continued to the warehouse if we didn't have so much business here, but it was still wonderful to stop and do something different.

The council had convened before we arrived and were talking about something in animated voices.

"What's happened?" I asked as they granted me an audience and heads turned my way.

"We've seen elves near here. Some are clearly aligned with Cherisse, and they have tried to attack our mythicals. They found one of our orbs and tried to make their way here with it."

I frowned, surprised but also puzzled. What did they want with the Sanctuary?

Instead of interrupting to ask my questions, I sat down and listened. I let them explain what they were debating. It was clear they were less concerned about why and more concerned with whether they should hide the Sanctuary and move again.

"Stay here," I said. "They'll find you no matter what you do and where you go if they truly want to. They're good at that, and they seem to have eyes and ears everywhere."

The council members all looked straight at me. I thought they were going to argue with me, but they deflated.

"I know you're used to moving away from danger, but this isn't one of those moments," I added in a gentler tone. "Now, why do they want to get into the Sanctuary?"

The councilors glanced at each other as if waiting for someone else to answer me

"We think they want the mythicals here. You've bonded with some impressive creatures and have shown that they are an effective bonus in battle, especially with the training you have done together."

I paused. It made sense, and I was surprised I hadn't put the information together. Having bonded mythicals was something I'd noticed they had lacked. Living in a mountain most of your life didn't make it easy to find and bond with creatures. On top of that, lots of the mythical creatures were in the Sanctuary, where it had been safer.

Sighing, I thought about how the mythicals could be protected while not being locked in since I had taken away some of the best fighting elves to guard the portal.

It was clear we needed to do something about Cherisse and consolidate the targets we were defending. She was divided, fighting on multiple fronts. It might be one way we could conquer her.

Voicing my thoughts, I presented the council with the idea that we might be able to use some of it to our advantage. It was detracting from the reason I was there—to talk about sending a spy into Cherisse's midst—but it wasn't the right time. I wasn't sure I had a choice, however.

"If we're going to tackle Cherisse on multiple fronts, it would help to know where she plans to aim first. Otherwise, we're dividing our forces and making it harder for ourselves."

I hesitated. I'd wanted to talk to Gwaelon and be sure first, but it seemed like I was going to have to talk about it now.

"What about sending an elf in as a spy?" I said. "One has volunteered, but it's dangerous."

"I think I know who that is," Ronan said, bowing to me.

I didn't confirm or deny. It wasn't my place to say

anything, and having as few people as possible know who the spy was would be a good idea.

The council moved on as if this settled everything.

Of course, I had more than one reason to want to use a spy now, but I wasn't going to talk about my other reason yet. While the Sanctuary council needed to know what was going on, they were more concerned with direct fights, and they were doing everything they could to defend a portal.

The other one was my burden to bear, and perhaps Gwaelon's.

Eventually, they reached a consensus. It was agreed that a spy would be useful, but like the other elves who were signed up to fight, it was important to everyone that the spy be a volunteer. Given I would never ask the water elf without him offering, I reassured them that it would be a volunteer and I would do no persuading.

This satisfied them and triggered the end of the meeting. The mythicals needed to be kept safe, and sitting around talking about it wasn't going to help.

I made my way straight to the area I thought I'd find the water elf, not wanting to leave it any longer. Although I was waylaid a couple of times by elves and sentient mythicals wanting to hear news of the elves at the portal or ask me how I was, I finally arrived at my destination. Zephyr, Roth, and Sen came with me, far more relaxed than I was.

To my surprise, I found Ronan was there. The strong centaur noticed me first.

"Forgive me," Ronan said. "I came without delay to check if your words were true. It wasn't meant as a lack of trust in you as much as my desire to be sure Gwaelon was serious about his intentions."

I bowed as centaurs did when they were showing someone respect. It was clear the council member thought highly of the water elf.

"You're in need of a spy after all?" Gwaelon asked. I filled him in on everything that had transpired that day and the previous one.

It wasn't an ideal situation to be in, and there was no way to do it without raising suspicions, but some risks we could mitigate. I planned to be nearby when Gwaelon contacted a group of Cherisse's elves and tried to convince them he was a turncoat.

After that, he would be on his own. I couldn't return to Mexico, and I couldn't watch his every move. He would have to hope they were all convinced. That said, I gave him all the info I could on the cult and what they cared about.

Ronan didn't leave right away. He listened to everything I had to say, and more than once, I found myself hoping he wouldn't be too angry. Although I'd told the council about what had happened in the mountain, I'd left some details out. I hid nothing, knowing any information might save Gwaelon's life.

When I was done, the water elf exhaled and ran a hand through his hair. It was clear I had overwhelmed him, and I wasn't sure what he made of it all. I worried that he'd change his mind, but instead, he looked at me a moment later with the steely light of determination in his eyes.

"If anyone can do this and get the information we need to finally stop these elves, I think I can. Thank you for telling me so much. It can't have been easy for you to live through all that."

I blinked, not sure how to respond. After everything I'd

said, I was pretty sure I should be thanking him for not walking away from the whole thing.

"Are you sure you want to do this?" I asked. I wouldn't want to.

"Yes. More sure than ever. And I'm aware that if the prophecy about you is right and unchangeable by our actions, I won't be successful. Not ultimately. But if there's a slim chance you will never be tested by the evil on the other side of the portals? If I can save you that. If I can save this world from the pain and destruction he'd bring to it or a few lives here, it's worth me trying."

I nodded, his words rendering me speechless. His conviction to this cause moved me. I'd thought I knew exactly who I was, but I was learning that there was always another layer. Another something to discover, flaws to fight, and passions to ignite.

Ronan was satisfied, but he didn't leave. Instead, he sat down and looked at me.

"It appears that we need to plan a meeting point and a suitable initial reason to want to join Cherisse and her fanatics." Ronan's voice was deep and calm despite the enormity of what he had said.

Gwaelon leaned forward, running his hand through his hair again. It wasn't an easy thing to think about. In the end, we had to make a decision, though.

"I think I know how and my approach," Gwaelon said. "She likes powerful elves and ones who are willing to do some pretty serious things in the name of the elven world. And she doesn't care who gets hurt or is punished. All she cares about is her goals and getting them done as swiftly as possible."

I nodded, not sure what else to add. It was all true and hard to fool and keep from doing anything that Gwaelon wouldn't normally do.

"Leave that part with me, then. I think I can make it happen. Let us worry about where she is and where we will find her. Do you think she'll make another attempt on the portal?"

As I thought about the answer to the question, I tilted my head to the side. Would she go for the portal again? She'd come close, but she'd lost elves, some of them locked in the cells on site now. I hadn't told the Sanctuary about that either yet. As much as they deserved to know, they also had shown they could be quite aggressive toward people they felt were against them in the past.

I'd had to advocate for the lives of some government agents who had been captured and stop the council from having them executed. While I wasn't sure they'd be that callous with their own kind, there was a chance they would. Or worse.

"I think she'll try the portal again if only to try to free some of her elves. While she doesn't like to rescue those who are weak, we've captured a lot."

"Good." Gwaelon's eyes lit up as he spoke. "Tell me about the captured elves. Tell me what happens to them and where they go. How likely is it that she'll rescue them?"

The questions came thick and fast, and I answered them to the best of my ability. This wasn't always easy, but I owed Gwaelon the truth, and it didn't take long for me to see where he was going with his questions. He wanted to be rescued as if he were one of them. To be in the prison with them.

Part of me wanted to point out that this happened frequently in the movies; it was common for someone to insert a spy into a group by having them appear as a prisoner in arms and then letting everyone be rescued. The government had tried something similar on us by sending a mythical to me under the guise of needing help to rescue his friends.

It was satisfying that he was dead and I had rescued the elves they had been holding from the government. Not all of them were grateful, but most were. The majority had slotted into life in the Sanctuary.

Of course, it had led to many other things, including a showdown on the lawn of the White House, but sometimes things escalated to the highest power in the land. It had forced me to go to the person who held the keys to the kingdom.

Despite my thoughts, I kept a straight face and offered to help Gwaelon. This would not be easy, and he needed all the help he could get.

Trying to be fair to the Sanctuary, it had been a while since there had been a threat. It was like they were rusty.

By the time we'd finished talking, we had a plan to insert Gwaelon into the group of Cherisse's elves. Then we had to hope they were rescued and make sure their escape was easy, but not too easy. The hard part was going to be persuading the President that sacrificing the prisoners was a good thing. We'd been making our odds of success higher as we captured more and more elves.

We needed to let them all go again.

CHAPTER SIXTEEN

With Gwaelon in tow, my team took to the skies once more. Although we'd not been long, partly to make sure Gwaelon didn't get cold feet and partly to get back to the portal before they attacked it again, we'd flown to the warehouse and checked in with everyone.

I still hadn't pursued the person whose photograph was in my package, but it had been good to chat with Lyra for a while and get a human's perspective on everything. She knew what I'd given, lost, and sacrificed for everyone already. She had known me from before I was a big prophecy elf. Before everyone started calling me Henera.

I'd come back to the Sanctuary to escort Gwaelon and had rested to regain my abilities before moving out. The water elf seemed happy enough to those who didn't know him well, but I could detect hints of fear and nerves in him. He was bound to be apprehensive, but I'd do what I could for him.

We were only going to travel a short way before I made it look as if he were my prisoner, an elf I'd captured to hand over to the government at the portal site. It probably wouldn't be necessary, but we might bump into Cherisse's elves along the way.

It had been Gwaelon's suggestion, and I wasn't going to argue, even if it slowed us down. If we were going to sell this, I was in all the way.

We slowly flew away from the Sanctuary, part of me feeling as if I would never go back. We'd lost Lorcan along the way, and what we were doing today made me think of it. Until that moment, I'd been fairly sure we'd all survive whatever we faced, but there was a chance that wasn't the case this time.

And facing Gwaelon's brother, the water master Ruehnar, if he didn't come back alive was going to be more than difficult. I didn't know how much Gwaelon had told him, but my dreams the previous night had been haunted by the thought of having to explain what he'd decided to do.

It was almost enough to make me call the whole thing off, but it wasn't down to me. The more I'd told Gwaelon, the more he had wanted to continue. There wasn't likely to be any turning back.

When we were far enough that we could execute the next part of our plan, I landed again, Zephyr having carried Gwaelon this far. We were going to have to make it look as if Gwaelon and I had fought and the water elf had suffered in the challenge.

Neither of us moved, aware this could easily hurt us. Water was my weakest element, and Gwaelon was about to challenge it. But I could also use the others, and he'd have very little he could do to stop me. It wasn't ideal, and we could break each other, but we had to make it look real.

I was still hesitating when Gwaelon sucked all the moisture out of the air and drew it toward him. It made it feel strange to breathe, and I didn't know what to do.

Zephyr roared, and Gwaelon flinched as the dragon took a step closer. Scared that my dragon might do something dangerous, I snapped out of the strange feeling that had settled on me and took another step forward, fighting for control of the water to return it to where it had been.

Either I had grown more efficient, or I took Gwaelon by surprise because I quickly smacked away his grip and pulled the water toward me. I felt better as I spread it out. Then I blasted the older elf off his feet. It was a powerful attack, and it smacked Gwaelon into a tree, rocking his body.

I winced, wondering if I'd gone too far, but he stood and straightened, then water rushed up from the ground and hit me in the back. What I'd taken for distraction and fear had been him concentrating.

Stumbling forward, I rocked the earth and controlled the plants as well. It was clear Gwaelon wasn't going to make this easy on me, and there was enough of me that relished the challenge that I reached for him with the plants.

Interestingly, he didn't try to dodge, letting me wrap vines around his arms and restrain him. Thinking I was done and Zephyr could step in and gas him, I relaxed. A moment later, however, he'd sucked all the moisture out of the plants, and they withered before my eyes. With ease, he snapped them and stepped forward again.

I felt a strange feeling inside as he tried to do the same with me. I felt as if I might panic, but I snapped out of it without needing Zephyr to roar at me. I fought for control of the water in my body, trying not to think about how Gwaelon had mimicked an attack I'd thought only the defense pillars around the portals could do.

I managed it, although it was harder to fight back than the last time. This wasn't an easy fight, but we'd agreed the mythicals would stay out of it unless I looked like I needed them. Right now, I still had the edge.

I wobbled Gwaelon again and made sure I had a strong grip on everything I needed, including the water in my body and the air around me. I wasn't going to let him blast me with anything else easily.

Gwaelon seemed to sense the resolve in me. I saw him almost give up, but then he attacked again, more water pouring out of the sky and drenching me in seconds.

I growled and decided to finish this, so I blasted him with all three elements I controlled. I used the falling water, the air along with it, and both shook the ground and grew more plants until Gwaelon was sinking into watery mud, the plants pulling him down while air blasted him so hard he was struggling to stay upright.

With a nod, I motioned to Zephyr to exhale as I dropped the wind and waited for his gas. The dragon obliged me, exhaling right over Gwaelon to make it easy for me. The elf couldn't move and barely tried to fight what we were doing. Within seconds, he was paralyzed.

The rain stopped, and I stepped up to him, moving the water, earth, and plants to pull him out of the ground.

"I'm sorry, friend. That wasn't easy, and I hope one day

we can laugh about it," I whispered as he came unstuck.

I floated him over to Zephyr, wondering how we'd make sure he didn't fall off and if I'd have to sit with him.

I'll carry him in a claw, Zephyr said. *It's the best way to make him look like a captive and not drop him.*

I wasn't entirely sure it was a great way for Zephyr to carry an elf for so many miles, but we didn't need to do anything else that day, and I couldn't think of a better solution to the problem.

Eventually, I nodded. *I'll fly beside to give you plenty of energy*, I added.

I thought Zephyr was going to object, but he didn't. He let me power into the air beside Roth and Sen, the duo together once more. While flying, I also boosted Roth a little, but not as much as I had done in the past. He was now stronger as well and finding his confidence. It had taken several weeks, and we'd put him in danger far more than I'd liked, but he was finally slotting into the team.

While we flew, I wondered what it would be like if I did gain the final element and introduce yet another mythical. I was surprised I had three, and it hadn't seemed difficult to find them to bond with. I knew many elves without a bonded creature. Was there a way to make it easier to find them?

I had no idea, but it was something to think about and talk to Minsheng about. If it did make the elves more powerful and Cherisse was trying to gain an advantage, it was worth looking into.

Tuviel and the other greats lived in a time when every elf had a bonded mythical. There were mythicals everywhere in my ancestors' memories, Zephyr said, sadness to his deep voice.

I sent warm thoughts his way to alleviate the sadness he felt, but I didn't interrupt him.

I'm not sure if there were more living then to bond with, but the elves all seemed to have them once they reached maturity and came into their abilities.

Then perhaps there is a way. If there are more of them, they are scattered across the entire planet. An elf in Asia might still have to travel to Europe to find their mythical, I replied without hesitation.

It's a good point to make. There must be a way to make it easier to find them. We should see if the organization or Sanctuary knows or could find something in our history to suggest that there's something that can guide people to mythicals they can bond with.

I exhaled, relieved that it wasn't an insane idea and Zephyr's memories backed it up. Of course, his memories weren't perfect, especially his older ones. I still marveled at how his mind could retain so much info without him going crazy, but he assured me it was as if each dragon's memories were tucked away in their space, and the space was infinitely large for them.

Grateful that I'd bonded with this amazing set of creatures, we flew on. When we were a few miles from the portal compound, I thought I saw some elves moving along the ground to the north, trying to hide but not doing a perfect job of it.

They didn't attack us, however, and I was pretty sure after my fight with Gwaelon and flying for several hours since that I didn't have a good fight in me. Not alone, anyway.

I was also worried that the elf would wake up soon. I

wasn't sure I could take on the skilled water elemental again. It was best to hand him over to the soldiers and be done with it.

Thankfully, the elves were soon behind us, and the compound came into view. I forgot about the elves and what they might be doing. They hadn't attacked us, and there was nothing out there they would be interested in.

As one, our group descended down to land outside, the soldiers waving and giving us space to touch down in the courtyard.

It was good to finally reach the destination. The flight had been tense because of the extra criteria and not knowing if we were going to be attacked. We'd arrived, however, and the soldiers rushed up, noticing the elf in Zephyr's claws.

The dragon placed him gently on the ground in front of the major.

"A friend?" he asked.

"No. One of hers. He attacked us on the way here, and we put him under. Put him with the other elves Cherisse sent," I said, hoping I sounded believable and feeling as if I'd lied so badly that it would be obvious.

The soldiers hurried forward to carry him away, however. Thankfully, they did it before anyone from the Sanctuary appeared and noticed he was one of their own.

Relaxing as we headed for the main building, where we could get food, I hoped we'd get a moment to calm ourselves down before something else happened. We were out of luck, however. and we hadn't been in the mess hall long before Minsheng appeared, the major with him.

I lifted my eyebrows but didn't speak since my mouth was full of food. They sat down in front of me.

"When you had to leave so swiftly, the President authorized your Shishou to have access to what we'd found and had flown in," the major explained.

"What was that?" I asked. I was ready for someone to explain.

"It's a stone tablet. Carved like the portals, but more...static," Minsheng said. "We can activate it similarly to the portals and pillars as far as I can tell."

I gulped. I didn't like what he was telling me, but I was aware there was a question on their faces. Did they want me to do something about it?

"Let me guess," I said. "It needs activating."

"Something like that." Minsheng shrugged apologetically.

I sighed and nodded.

"All right. I need to see the President about something if he's here. If not, whoever is in charge at the moment. Then I will come help you with whatever you need."

The major got up as if he were going to object, but he nodded.

"I'll go see if the colonel will see you. It's likely he will, but if he's difficult about it, I'll make sure he sees sense."

I grinned as the major strode off. I was thankful that we'd had the confrontation and then been forced to sort it out. It had changed everything, and I now had one of my first true allies in the human-run military. It was clear I needed all the allies I could get.

As I was finishing, the major came back and gave me a nod.

"When you're ready, I will take you to him. I think he's excited to meet Zephyr, Roth, and Sen too. He's heard a lot about you."

I exhaled, relieved that we were likely to find another friend if nothing else. Or at least someone who was starting with a positive attitude.

Zephyr, Roth, and Sen came with me, and I could feel lighter emotions coming off them. I was grateful they were faring better, but I knew it was likely to be a brief respite. We had a lot to work through and an enemy who was going to keep coming.

The major led us toward the small office the President had used to get us to explain our fight. It was a shock, but there was a thin gray-haired man sitting behind the desk, looking at something on his computer.

He glanced up as the major showed me in.

"Thank you, Major. I'll come find you when I'm done here. It's best that what I say is known by as few people as possible. It gives it a greater chance of success." I tried not to sound mysterious, but the major winked and left, shutting the door behind us.

Zephyr struggled to fit in, but we were soon positioned around the desk, Sen on my shoulder and the colonel on his feet, his eyes shining with delight at seeing us.

"It's a pleasure to meet you, Colonel," I said as I put out my hand to shake his.

He pumped it enthusiastically, then offered to shake hands with the others. I enjoyed being greeted once again with dignity and respect, then I got down to business. The next time Cherisse came, things were going to have to be different.

CHAPTER SEVENTEEN

I was flying on Zephyr's back and watching the sunset. We were scouting around the portal site, helping guard it, and we had been for several days. Although we'd made plans and knew what to do if Cherisse showed up to get at the portal or rescue her elves, we'd barely seen anything of the elven cult.

Now and then, the soldiers or elves protecting the base had patrolled outward and come back with an elf they'd captured, but never more than one or two at a time.

I didn't think for a second that Cherisse had gone away and the problem had solved itself. She was out there somewhere, planning another attack, and I had to be ready for it. That assumed she hadn't found a way to open the portal in the mountain with the team she had.

Of course, it did seem as if this larger portal was easier to open, especially if someone was on the other side and connected, but I didn't know how much easier. I'd tried once to see if the pillars could be destroyed only.

It brought my mind to the tablet with symbols on it that

Minsheng was studying. I hadn't been able to activate that either. It didn't respond. As if it were dormant. And no one else knew about it still. I had tried to suggest we ask the organization or Sanctuary about its possible purpose and how to activate it, but the government wasn't ready for that yet.

I suspected they were also aware that it didn't belong to the government but the elves, not to mention that no one knew what it did. For all they knew, it could be a bomb. They were unlikely to hand that over to a race or group they knew little about and were just beginning to trust.

Zephyr had searched his memories, but the information that he'd seen something like it was the best he could offer. Whatever it was, it was yet another mystery in my life.

Just like my parents, and how Zephyr's egg had been in a warehouse waiting for me. A warehouse I had owned my entire life without realizing. And how I could use more than one element, as well as so many other things.

Someone out there had the answers I needed, and I was going to find them as soon as I could.

We'll find them. Together, Zephyr said as he swooped around and lower. *One at a time until we understand. And we'll do it all while protecting those we care about and being badass.*

I heard the chuckle in his voice and couldn't help but laugh. Zephyr never failed to make me feel better about everything. We were going to do what we needed one task at a time.

Roth and Sen were running about the outside space by the time we flew back and landed, the water pegasus sparkling in the dying light. I slid off Zephyr's back and went to them, smiling at their antics and feeling better they were close.

I was also thankful that Roth had come along and provided a companion for Sen. I was bonded with all of them in the same way, but Zephyr held my heart as well, and sometimes it made for awkward conversation or a need for privacy I didn't always want.

Those were worries for another day, however, and I didn't plan to heap more on my shoulders when I still had so many more pressing ones. It was almost time to rest, my watch mostly during the day despite the increased likelihood that Cherisse would show up at night. I trained the others during the day, and I didn't want anyone to get used to me being here to help. I couldn't stay for long.

I was still in the front courtyard with them, all of us running and playing a magic enhanced game of tag when Minsheng appeared. He had a laptop in his hands and a grin on his face.

When he came closer, I got the impression he had something to show me, but we were still a hundred feet from each other when he was blasted with air and knocked to the ground. The laptop went flying as I rushed over to him, reaching to control the elements around us as the soldiers yelled for backup and took up defensive positions.

I helped Minsheng to his feet, grateful he didn't appear to be injured. The laptop was shattered, however, the screen cracked and a swirl of colors. He tried to pick it up as Zephyr flew up to find the source of the attack. Sen bounded onto my shoulder.

Minsheng didn't get to the laptop before he was driven back and had to find shelter.

As Roth came in and the soldiers filed out of the main barracks, I felt someone reaching to control the earth to one side. It wasn't a strong reach, more someone tentatively feeling for what I controlled to take some if it was useful.

I wondered if others had felt me in a similar way, but it was the first time I'd felt it. Was this new? Something I'd only recently learned to do?

Having no idea, I tried not to focus on it, instead looking for the threat. Someone was out there, but where were they, and how many elves were with them?

I didn't have to wonder for long. A group of elves came rushing out of a hole in the ground, the earth shaking as vines snaked out with them. This was going to be one big battle.

Not wanting to waste the opportunity and advantage I had to start, I hurled air at the first few ranks as they appeared, knocking them back and taking some of the elves behind down with them. Zephyr roared to one side, drawing my gaze and showing me that more elves were rushing toward the large building that housed the elven prisoners at the site.

Part of me fought to do nothing about it, wanting to let them rescue their prisoners and Gwaelon along with them, but I couldn't let it be that easy. Instead, I yelled to alert the soldiers.

We'd done everything we could to make it so they'd escape. We had to make it look like it was their skill and we weren't helping. Zephyr looped around again as Roth and some of the soldiers ran toward the prison. I tried to follow but the vines snaked closer, grabbing soldiers and guns to prevent them from shooting more elves.

I stopped again and reached for the plants with my mind. They were held by several earth elves, their minds strong and determined, but I managed to bat away their control and take the vines in hand. I put down the soldiers, unwrapped the vines from the weapons, and shriveled them up.

It took most of my concentration to keep going as the elves tried to wrest control from me. Once each vine was a lifeless husk, I let go, feeling guilt for killing a perfectly good plant but aware we were outnumbered and if the prisoners escaped, it would only get worse.

On top of that, our elves were mostly in the portal cavern, making sure it was defended. I was proud of how well they'd come together, but they couldn't do this without me making it easier for them.

Focusing and hoping Zephyr, Sen, and Roth could make it look as if the prison were the priority, I continued to work with the soldiers. The major appeared nearby, calling orders as he sheltered with Minsheng behind one corner of a building and took shots at the elves. Twice I had to stop something from hitting him, like water seeming to come out of nowhere.

Now and then, something was flung at me or the ground beneath my feet was attacked, but I held firm, my training making it hard for the elves I fought to snatch control from me when I was distracted. The vines kept coming, however. It felt as if for every one I killed and let go of, another two grew.

I growled as yet another appeared, creeping down the

side of the building toward the major and Minsheng. The broken laptop still lay on the ground, forgotten by everyone but me until I noticed a small sand-colored plant was creeping closer to it.

Did they want what was on the device? I had no way to be sure, but I would not take any chances. I stepped closer to it and forced out the elf controlling it. More elves bombarded me, trying to take it back, but I doubled it back on itself, the plant hardier than the vines everywhere else.

When another powerful earth elf pushed my control away again, I winced, stepping back as if they had slapped me. It had hurt, and it was most likely the earth elf who had been with Cherisse when they'd last attempted to open the portal. The plants started growing toward the laptop again.

Frustrated and angry that they had attacked Minsheng because of the tech he was carrying, I used the air I controlled to blast the laptop farther away and looked for something I could hack at the plant with. It would help if I could let them waste their magic while I used physical means.

The major chucked a knife my way, the blade in a leather pouch strapped to the handle as if he sensed what I wanted to do. A moment later, a blast of air almost knocked him off his feet. I cushioned him with air and spun him back to safety. As soon as he was walking under his own power again, I gave him a nod and grabbed the knife.

After drawing it, I slashed at the plant, cutting off the main runner and stomping on it. At the same time, I kept a grip on the air around me and the earth at my feet. A box protected me while I stood out in the open. With the plant well and truly dead, I looked for somewhere safe to put the laptop.

Minsheng reached for it, but I shook my head. For whatever reason, they wanted this computer, and while the data on it might be recoverable, whoever held it would be in danger. There was no way I was giving it to someone who couldn't defend themselves.

I felt a stab of pain a moment later and looked down at my leg, expecting to see something sticking out of it. When I realized I was fine, I looked toward the prison block and my mythicals.

Zephyr, Sen, Roth, are any of you hurt? I asked, focusing on them as I defended myself.

It was me, Roth replied. *Got my leg stuck in something. I'm free, and I'll be fine again in a minute or two.*

I exhaled, grateful as the pain faded. There were more questions in my mind, but the elves had reached the perimeter fence despite the soldiers firing at them, and many were still caught up in vines. If that many enemy elves got close to me, I was going to be in big trouble.

Once more, I set about taking control of the vines, killing them and letting their prisoners go. I wondered if they were rescuing their people now. Slowly, I freed enough soldiers, and they shot enough elves to turn the tide, the air elves focusing on retrieving those sedated while I decimated the rest of the vines.

Eventually, they gave up growing more, my mind still working fast enough and with enough skill that I'd begun killing them faster than my counterpart could replenish them. Then an elf broke my grip, rocking the ground beneath my feet or blasting me with air or water.

I kept my place, defending as many of the soldiers as I could and keeping myself safe.

I think they're trying to pull back, Zephyr said a moment later. *Some of them are spent, and the soldiers here are still putting up a reasonable fight.*

Are the prisoners free?

Some, but not many. I've not seen Gwaelon.

I frowned. That wasn't good news. If they didn't rescue Gwaelon, he had no chance as a spy.

Can you pretend to be injured? I asked a moment later.

Not convincingly. No one is getting close enough to hurt me anymore.

Before I could think of anything else or get the major's attention to see if we could pull more soldiers to help us, there was a small explosion from the side of the prison building.

There was also a renewed effort by the elves to take control of the elements around me. It seemed they'd realized they hadn't freed their prisoners and were going to make sure of it.

While I defended myself, the soldiers were battered. It gave the major a reason to call more soldiers away from the prisoners. I worried that we'd be overwhelmed, but Seth appeared at my side, hurling fire and slipping into the area I protected alongside me.

"Looks like you could use a hand," he said, grinning from ear to ear.

"The portal?"

"They only attacked it halfheartedly. It wasn't their goal

today. As soon as they started pulling back, I knew we could risk taking a few elves out and bringing them out here. I can sense your control and you slinging stuff around from miles away these days."

I lifted my eyebrows at Seth's words, but an elf took that moment to challenge my control again. With Seth protected by me as well, I had to focus on keeping us safe. But that freed him up to attack.

While he was slinging fire and there were extra soldiers, we recovered our advantage again. More of the elves seemed to run out of power and pull back and then the fight was over. They slunk away, heading back down the tunnels they'd created.

I didn't relax, keeping the control I had and moving forward. Seth came with me, helping the soldiers catch another couple of elves by setting fires in their path and giving the men another chance to hit them with trank darts.

There was something strange about seeing the weapons that had once been used on us targeting other elves, but I was grateful they weren't using lethal force.

Eventually, we were alone. The soldiers regrouped as my mythicals returned to my side. Several of the soldiers were injured and some had nasty burns. I wished I had the power to heal and not the ability to control three elements. Sadly, I could only cause damage. Stopping it or fixing things with my abilities was far harder.

When Minsheng came over, I checked Roth and his injury. My Shishou fetched the laptop, making me wonder what was so important on it and what had happened. He didn't say anything, but his shoulders slumped as he surveyed the damage that had been done to it.

I tried to focus on my mythicals despite my curiosity, wanting Roth to know I cared that he'd been hurt.

I'm fine now, he said when I ran my hands over the leg the pain had emanated from. *As good as new, although I would love a saltwater bath to be sure.*

Anything you need, I replied before asking one of the uninjured soldiers who was composed and on duty if someone could help us by getting him a saltwater bath. The soldier seemed to perk up at seeing me.

"Oh, my...days. It's her. You're *her*. And you're so much more adorable in person. I feel as if I could tuck you under one arm and keep you safe. Is that what you need? Safety. Because there's a lot of well-trained soldiers here and a bunch of other elves, too."

I blinked, surprised by the strange waffle the soldier had spewed at me. It was more than confusing and made me hesitate before asking for the saltwater bath again and drawing the soldier's attention to Roth.

A moment later, the soldier turned to Roth and gaped as if he'd only just realized the pegasus was standing beside me. Zephyr came closer and lowered his head down by my side.

When the soldier stepped back, he jumped. Zephyr was almost in the soldier's personal space.

"Aella and I have a very close bond, and it makes it very easy for me to take care of her needs, but if you're offering, I could eat about ten large pepperoni pizzas," Zephyr said, his voice a touch deeper than normal and very slow and deliberate.

The guy nodded, looking scared, then backed up a little.

I tried not to laugh as I asked for pizzas for Roth, Sen, and me, then hurried toward the barracks and the room we'd been assigned. I needed to rest. Everything else could wait.

CHAPTER EIGHTEEN

As Ronan walked beside my mythicals and me, the presence of my favorite centaur calmed me as it had for most of the time he'd known me. I'd told him what had happened at the portal and we'd talked about how the plan had gone and how we'd finally been able to do certain things.

He wasn't an elven master, so he didn't understand how my powers worked, but centaurs had a magic all their own, and he seemed to use it frequently to calm my emotions when I was with him. Centaurs could also tie themselves to a certain type of stone and use them to communicate over large distances.

There wasn't a single moment I'd had with Ronan where I hadn't come away a better person or calmer, or more positive. He was an amazing influence in my life, and he always had time for me.

"It sounds as if a storm is coming. One we need to be prepared for," he said after a moment.

"I believe so. Cherisse isn't going to give up, and we're standing in her way."

"As we should. But we must ensure we don't get washed away. Our forces are scattered, and we find ourselves protecting more and more. It is right that we do so, but if we're not careful, we can easily be overcome."

"I understand that. I feel as if I spend more of my time flying between the warehouse, the portal, and here than I do helping anywhere. And I still worry that I cannot help them all enough."

"You have trained many, and the elven masters here continue to do so. Our best fighters are at the portal, and Seth has been learning command for some time under my guidance. The warehouse is likely to need you most should the worst happen, and it would be right for you to defend your own home. You should never feel guilty for that. We will all fight better defending what we care most about."

I nodded, once more grateful for Ronan's wisdom. There was one more thing to bring to his attention, however.

With a flourish, I pulled out the photo of the strange stone tablet and showed it to the centaur. He stopped walking and took it to look more closely.

"It reacts to the portal, according to Minsheng. He took it there on a whim after I couldn't seem to activate it."

"Yes. It would. It's an old elemental focusing stone, designed to help an elf learn their abilities and focus on them or help teachers know what element an elf is most likely to master. It's not perfectly accurate since it takes on a marker similar to how you describe the control of the elements and the trace it leaves behind. In short, it only finds elves with control similar to the maker's. If my memory serves, it also absorbs and stores elemental energy, like a memory."

I listened in stunned disbelief, wondering how much other technology and how many strange artifacts like this were lying around, and how much I still didn't know.

"We thought these were broken or destroyed long ago. They were used by...him. He gathered elves with the same mindset around him who could all control in a similar way, and it made him more formidable. I wouldn't be surprised if Cherisse and her cult want one or have at least one."

The thought chilled me, but I didn't think Ronan was wrong. If this device did what he said, it explained why Cherisse and her elves had been trying to get the laptop and the data on it. But how did they know about it? Minsheng and I only knew from the mythicals at the portal site. Did we have a spy as well?

It doesn't explain why it reacted to the portal, Zephyr pointed out, taking another step beside me. His eyes were on the horizon, making it appear as if he weren't saying anything to me.

I repeated Zephyr's words aloud, hoping he didn't mind me echoing them to Ronan. The centaur looked thoughtful.

"I wonder..." Ronan retrieved the photo. "Do you have a photograph of the pillars by any chance?"

I didn't, but a quick message to Minsheng on my phone resulted in one a minute later. Lifting my phone, I held it beside the photo of the tablet and let Ronan get a good look. There were very similar symbols on them, and they had possibly been carved from the same type of rock, but that could have been a coincidence.

"I believe this reacted to the portal because the same elf made it, or one very similar," Ronan said a moment later.

It would explain a lot, Zephyr added. *And if that's the case, it makes the tablet ancient. The pillars have been there for at least two millennia.*

This was almost more information than I could handle, and I wasn't sure what to do with it.

As I thought about it, I realized it could easily have been one of my ancestors. One of the great elves. But if that was the case, why didn't it respond to me? Why hadn't I been able to turn it on?

I had no idea, but I wanted to try again with the wisdom I now possessed. I thanked Ronan and was about to leave him to his day when a strange look came over his face. He reached out to me and, not sure what else to do, I placed my hand in his.

We were standing in the dark room that housed our minds when using the communication stones the centaurs bonded with. Opposite us was Gwaelon.

"Ronan," he said, bowing to the centaur and then to me, Zephyr, Sen, and Roth. "And Aella and all your wonderful mythicals. My gratitude to see you all here. There is much wisdom you can provide, and it makes my heart glad to see you."

"Are you all right?" the centaur asked, beating me to the question by a fraction of a second. Gwaelon appeared well, but I knew a person coming into something like this had some control over their appearance. Zephyr always appeared in dragon form, even when he was in human form.

"I shouldn't take long to explain, but yes. I appear to have been accepted. It's enough to give me a place to work, food, and some elves to talk to. I suspect I won't find out lots yet, but they're beginning to let me in. And they haven't done anything to hurt me."

"This is good news in and of itself," Ronan continued as I nodded, relaxing.

"It is something to be grateful for, for sure. But I have other news. It's clear Cherisse is planning something. The elves here are all preparing for something big, and I think they plan to divide their forces to hit multiple targets at once. Divide and conquer and hope to weaken you all enough that nothing will stop them from opening the portal."

"The Texas portal?" I asked, stepping forward.

"I believe so," Gwaelon replied. "The portal here has a strange, almost religious significance, but it's very strongly protected and so dormant that opening it will be harder. There's something they're not telling me, but I can feel it."

I sighed. It was good news. No part of me wanted to go back to the mountain the other portal was in. If it wasn't a portal this group of elves thought they could handle, it made my task easier, and it was one less place I had to worry about.

"We'll fortify all three locations," I said as Gwaelon looked at us. "Let us know if you learn anything else we can use, but otherwise, stay safe and keep your head down. If it looks like they suspect you, leave."

The water elf nodded, gratitude lighting his eyes. Then

the connection disappeared and I returned to my mind, blinking in the bright sunlight beside Ronan.

Slowly Ronan let go of me, and we both exhaled. It was always a surreal experience to have my mind connect with another via a centaur stone, and this time had been no different. Cherisse was doing exactly what we'd feared she would, and we'd given her a significant portion of her army back.

Had we played straight into her hands?

It's possible, Zephyr said. *But we did what we thought was right at the time. It's all we can do.*

He was correct, but it didn't make me feel better. I wanted to know we could survive this—that I hadn't made it impossible.

We might have to permanently remove the threat if it comes to that. Letting them go again, keeping them locked up. Eventually, they'll grow powerful enough to succeed no matter what we do. No one wins all the time.

Zephyr's words sent a chill through me. We'd never killed our kind, and it had been a long time since we'd killed a human, let alone deliberately. It wasn't going to be easy to do something like that. Could we?

If it stops them from opening the portal, we might have to.

But we don't know for sure that opening the portal will be bad. We could be killing someone for no good reason, and that makes us as bad as them if not worse, I replied, feeling sick. I was aware that Ronan was staring at Zephyr and me as we looked at each other.

Do we not know? There's clearly something on the other side. It might not be him, but it could be.

It could. But killing another elf, even a misguided one...I don't think I can do it.

Could you defend yourself if one was trying to kill you? The concern in Zephyr's voice was intense enough that my mouth fell open, but I considered his question.

Yes, I think so, I said honestly. *If it came to it, I could kill someone if they gave me no other choice and it was that or let myself or someone I cared about die.* I thought about Lorcan and how I'd have happily killed the agent who'd ended his life.

Then that is enough. I would do the same for you. Zephyr lowered his head and looked me in the face. His eyes said everything. He would kill for me, and I would kill for him. We'd die for each other too. I hoped it never came to the latter.

"Do I need to give you two time to talk?" Ronan asked. "It seems you have something important to discuss, and I know the bond you share can both help and hinder this process. I wouldn't want to make anything harder on either of you."

"No, it's okay. We're in agreement on what matters," I replied.

"We should go to the council and let the rest of them know that we need to make the Sanctuary more defensible until we have deterred Cherisse once and for all," Zephyr added, the serious tone in his voice making it deeper.

I nodded. We had to start somewhere, and I had a feeling they needed the most convincing to prepare properly. The soldiers were trying to make the portal safer, and I was going to be in charge of everything at the warehouse. The council was another matter.

Ronan agreed with our suggestion, and we made our way to the center of the Sanctuary and the caverns that held the most important elements of the city.

Sierrathen was walking in the sun with Ruehnar as we approached, deep in discussion. They smiled when they saw us.

"We've had news," Ronan said as he bowed respectfully to the elder elves.

They looked at each other and back at us.

"We will convene the council, and Ruehnar, you may join us if you wish. This is likely to be about your brother, and I know you care greatly for him. We wouldn't keep anything about him from you, nor our decisions regarding his knowledge and safety."

I nodded, grateful for Sierrathen's insight and her care for the elves in her city. It was the right thing to do.

There was nothing more to be said as we made our way inside the cave, the light reflecting around it and making it beautiful. I made a mental note to see if we could get a similar system for the portal room. It was lit by floodlights and manmade constructions, but it wasn't the same. And the elves could protect their mirrors and panels.

More than once, the attacking elves had broken lights, barriers, and anything else they could. While there had been plenty more, and they'd always been fixed or replaced quickly, something that protected itself had an advantage.

I didn't get another opportunity to think about it, however, since more of the council arrived, hurrying as if they had been told something urgent needed their attention. Within ten minutes, we were all sitting at the council table, a light brunch laid out and extra seats brought in for Ruehnar and my mythicals.

I let Ronan take the lead, knowing his words would carry more weight and that I was more of a witness to what had transpired. I might have agreed to let Gwaelon become the spy we needed, but I'd only been involved because he'd needed my help, and I could aid him. Control of this didn't lie with me, and I hoped never to have an ego big enough to claim it.

It didn't take long for Ronan to tell the council everything, but silence followed the information. Finding out an attack was coming was not easy to hear. I had a feeling the Sanctuary had never faced that possibility while the current council was alive until I had come along.

The only other time they'd faced attack, they had moved the Sanctuary, and we'd ambushed the attackers before they could reach the city. It had resulted in the death of several elves, but the city had been safe in its current location ever since. I had a feeling that the council worried they would lose more people if they didn't move again.

"This is quite the problem," Sierrathen said, the first to find her voice.

That was an understatement since it was a tremendous problem, and there wasn't an easy way around it.

"I will help make the city more defensible. Use my earth magic to raise natural defenses and anything else the minds here can think of," I said when no one spoke.

"I appreciate the offer. Especially when, if I understand this correctly, the attack will also be upon your home,"

Vestan replied, his hand going to the female elf's resting on the arm of the chair beside him.

"It will. My home has been modified to make it more defensible. It has withstood more than one attack in the last few years." It wasn't the entire truth, but it would suffice.

This seemed to help the council, although I could see many of them were still nervous. No one wanted to face battle if they didn't have to, and they were uninclined to do so.

Thankfully, Ruehnar and Ronan were looking at each other.

"I can work with the other elven masters to see what we can do. The warning could make all the difference. They'll have no idea what they're walking into and we'll be able to make sure our elves and the many other mythicals with skills and talents of the right nature are ready." Ruehnar got to his feet as if this settled everything.

Martyl frowned and shook his head.

"I'm not sure this is wise. We don't know what we're up against and we can move the city. We've done it many times. It would prevent them from finding us in time."

"Normally I would agree with you, Martyl, but not this time," Vestan replied. "We are not hiding from the humans of this world or trying to divert one of their attacks. These are other elves. Our usual protections won't work. They have proven they are adept at finding the orbs, and they only need to get close to then be drawn to us. No. We need to prepare for a battle as best we can."

"We can deactivate the orbs," Nesryn the gnome said.

I frowned, wanting to point out that it wouldn't help, or

ask for how long they planned to hide like that, but Ronan very diplomatically said something similar.

For several minutes I sat back, reaching for Zephyr, Roth, and Sen with my mind to soothe their emotions as well as my own while the council argued. Normally they were in agreement, and I was the one who was trying to convince them of something, but I didn't have to this time.

Before too much longer had passed, it was clear. There was only one option. The Sanctuary had to prepare for war.

CHAPTER NINETEEN

As the outskirts of LA came into view, I felt a surge of relief. I had missed being at the warehouse and was grateful to finally be heading back there. I was sitting on Zephyr's back, with Sen sleeping in my jacket. Roth was flying in Zephyr's slipstream, aided by me.

We'd stuck around at the Sanctuary for another day after the council made their minds up and began creating extra layers of defense to aid them. Although we'd helped where we could, I'd been aware that I needed most of my power for whatever would follow and for making the warehouse extra-secure. I'd also had to have several meetings over secure internet connections with government officials.

The President had wanted to speak to me again to know what I knew and how much I trusted the information. He'd pointed out that it could be a bluff, something that would make us divide ourselves more. He was right. It could be many different things, and we had no way to be sure.

But we needed to do something, and if it encouraged us to create better defenses at the three sites, it wasn't a bad thing. I smiled as I thought about what Cherisse would find if she did attack again. We were making it a lot harder, and I had more than a few tricks up my sleeve.

Zephyr flew the last few miles, heading for the warehouse as if it were a beacon calling him home. He landed on the roof with ease, then folded his large wings back in toward his body. I noticed Roth landed well beside him, looking less tired than he had on other trips we'd made. He was stronger and more used to the life we led. We all were.

Daisy and Lyra met us as we descended into the heart of the building, my mind reaching out and feeling for the state of the stone and bricks that made up the walls and foundations. They weren't perfect, some of the work I'd done with my earth powers crumbling here and there, but it had been one of my first attempts to make a building strong.

I'd pulled up rock from the surrounding area, packing it more tightly together and fusing it with the walls of the warehouse. It had gone from a brick building to one made of that and a single piece of stone, and it had changed everything about the structure. I'd had to make sure the foundations could hold it all.

Given how much I'd pulled from the surrounding area, I was also aware I'd weakened the land around the building. A few cracks had appeared in the road and the foundations of the neighboring buildings. Those had to be fixed as well. As much as I wanted my warehouse to stand, I needed to make sure I didn't hurt anyone else or their property in the process. But first, I needed to get everyone else up to speed.

Since then, I'd gained several earth elves, a couple from the Sanctuary and others from around the world who had traveled to train under me and be kept safe in difficult situations. Normally Emily and Daisy were around to help take care of all the elves living here, but Emily was visiting her mother, and I had no idea when she'd be back.

I'd told Daisy and Minsheng everything that was happening and Ronan's theory about the tablet. It was going to be an interesting few days, if nothing else.

Daisy ushered me downstairs, where she'd just prepared a meal. I was famished and grateful to find that everyone else was there, also tucking into the food. We were going to need all the power we could get.

"I had a chat with some of the dojo students. The ones who've gotten their heads screwed on straight and know all about you and what you can do. There's a bunch of volunteers to help defend the place and all of the mythicals here," Lyra said as I sat down with a heaping bowl of chow mein.

I lifted my eyebrows, surprised that humans were considering helping us. This was an elven war.

"Can you get us more dart guns from your contacts in the military?" she continued.

My mouth fell open when I realized I hadn't thought of asking the US military for help with defending my home. They might help the Sanctuary as well. They had plenty of sentient mythicals who could be taught to wield a weapon. It didn't hurt to ask.

I grabbed my cell phone and sent a quick message to

Minsheng, hoping asking through my Shishou would work. He was the one at the portal helping the human scientists with their side project. It might work better coming from him, and it was worth asking regardless.

Lyra seemed satisfied and went back to eating what was left of her food since one of her classes was starting soon.

The rest of the elves ate more slowly and in larger quantities than normal, all of us storing energy for the magic we'd need to modify the building further. I had quite a few ideas, and it turned out that Daisy had some of her own.

Within minutes of eating, we'd divided up the teams of elves, all of us having something to do to create defenses for the building and all of us eager. It was strange to look at the group of elves with me and think about how far we'd come, but this wasn't the time for speeches. We needed to get on with the changes.

While Zephyr, Roth, and Sen helped explain some of the plan to the other mythical creatures also in the building, I got to work. Going up to the roof, I sat in the middle of it with the other earth elves, feeling outward and trying not to bump into each other as we worked on sections.

I started with repairs, fixing cracks, crumbling parts, and anything else that felt as if it needed reinforcing. While I was doing that, one of the earth elves with me worked on adding some extra layers, hollowing out the rock and stone where I'd made it far thicker than it needed to be, and removing the brick that was entirely unhelpful.

The two earth elves with me worked on the foundation, making sure it was strong and both air- and watertight. We couldn't have any cracks in the system. At least not yet.

It felt like it took almost no time, banter passing back and forth as we worked. Then an elf of another element joined us to play their part. I switched from moving rock and stone and plants to controlling water and air. In reality, we were up on the roof long into the night, shaping and creating and planning more for another day.

By the time we were all spent, each elf being sent to rest the moment they could give no more, I got to my feet. Despite my multitasking and the enormity of the part I'd played, I was the last elf still going, only my mythicals and the fire salamanders still keeping me company.

Zephyr leaned into me, tired as well. I was grateful for his support as I wobbled, momentarily dizzy. I'd pushed myself to my limits, coming close to losing the feeling of my bonded mythicals with how drained I'd become.

You need rest before we face another day, Zephyr said. He was stating the obvious, but it was sweet of him to care so much.

I looked at the stars above us.

It's been a while since we've been awake so late at night. We've drifted back to being active during the day now that we're not hiding from anyone.

That's the way it's supposed to be, but I do miss the quiet of night with you. Like this. Or on a beach, or flying through the night sky together.

I miss it sometimes too, although I don't miss the hiding and running from danger.

Me neither, Zephyr said as he slowly morphed from a dragon into his human form. Now a strong, good-looking man stood beside me. I was still leaning into him, and his arm came around me as I rested my head on his chest.

I exhaled, relaxing and feeling safe. It was a perfect moment since I realized Sen and Roth were fast asleep and the fire salamanders had slunk off to their beds as well. It was just the two of us staring at the stars.

Despite how tired I was, I didn't want to sleep yet. Zephyr seemed to have similar ideas. After a moment of simply holding me, he leaned in and pressed a kiss to my lips.

My heart skipped a beat as my passion rose. Zephyr had been by my side through everything, and I loved him. We focused on each other, our minds and hearts one.

Sighing as Zephyr pulled away, I took his hand and led him to our bedroom.

We spent two more days fortifying the warehouse before we had everything as we wanted it. We'd experienced problems storing water. There were tiny cracks we'd not noticed or that had formed since we'd worked on other sections, letting it out slowly. We soon had those fixed as well.

I hadn't used up all my reserves since the first day, wanting to have something in me if Cherisse surprised us, but so far, we had been left alone.

I'd talked to Minsheng and Ronan every day, all of us using the centaur communication stones to enter one mind room and converse about our plans and the changes taking place at each of the three locations.

Zephyr came with me, but we let Roth and Sen rest,

knowing they were going to be taxed the most by any battle.

There was little to report. Everyone was warier as time passed, especially since Gwaelon hadn't checked in with us again, but there was nothing any of us dared to do. Ronan wasn't willing to risk exposing Gwaelon by reaching out to his stone instead of waiting, and I'd never have asked him to.

All we could do was make ourselves as ready as possible.

"I've done more tests on the tablet," Minsheng said on the third day.

I lifted my eyebrows but didn't speak, wondering what he'd found. We'd passed on everything Ronan had said, and the centaur had answered more questions during the meetings we held each day, but it had yielded nothing so far.

"We took it near the portal again as you suggested, but we tried different pillars this time. It responds better to one than it does to the other three. A lot better. It might be the only one it's interacting with," Minsheng explained.

"Which one?" I asked.

"I don't know what elements they each control, but the back one on the right."

"Fire." That explained why I couldn't do anything with the tablet. It wasn't my element.

Everyone nodded, lost in thought as we processed the information

"Does Seth know about it yet?" I asked a few seconds later.

Minsheng shook his head. "They don't want to give him

security clearance until they know it can't be used to make the portal easier to open."

"It might," Ronan said, sadness in his voice. "But I will vouch for Seth. I've known him his whole life. He would never betray the elves in the Sanctuary. He'll not use it, and he'll protect its secret."

"You don't have to convince me, but the government takes their time."

"Say I'll vouch for him as well," I added, feeling weird saying it but aware it had come out instinctively. I trusted Seth, and I appreciated him being on my side in battle. If Ronan trusted him as well, it was enough.

"I'll make sure they know. And I'll let you know if we make any more progress."

"Have they let you know where they found it?" Ronan asked. "The council is very interested."

"They claim it was in an archaeological dig somewhere in Texas, but they're being...*cagey* about it. I don't think I'm being told the truth."

"I'll see if I can get the information," I added, although I wasn't sure how. As interesting as it was, it wasn't our highest priority. Not now, anyway.

There was nothing else to say. Cherisse hadn't been seen in several days, and neither had any of her elves. We had to be on our guard. There was no way she wasn't planning something, but we would just have to wait and watch.

And make sure we were prepared.

CHAPTER TWENTY

Standing on the edge of the warehouse, I watched the sunset. Zephyr was beside me in dragon form, gazing at the sky as it changed hue and darkened.

Below us were elves, dwarves, gnomes, and humans, all living in harmony, most ready to defend their home. The government had come through for us and the Sanctuary, providing plenty of dart guns and ammunition as well as other items we needed. There was little more we could do now but wait.

Minsheng let Daisy know they spotted some elves on patrol today. They appeared to be preparing for battle, Zephyr said a moment later.

Then it will probably happen tonight, I replied. *Get all the elves to rest but be ready for battle. And have the dwarves and gnomes keep an eye out.*

You should rest as well.

I will, right after we've done one thing.

What do you have in mind?

Stuffing our faces with pizza.

A grin broke out on Zephyr's face as I turned away from the sky and made my way back inside the warehouse. If we were going to be fighting for our lives soon and had some warning, I didn't see why we couldn't eat our favorite post-fight food before instead of after. It wouldn't be the first time we'd done so. One of our first battles had been preceded by pizza.

Zephyr followed, both of us telling whoever we saw that battle was likely before dawn and getting them to spread the word. Sen and Roth came too, the magic word echoing through our connection summoning them.

Holfin had anticipated us, and he pulled a hot, fresh pizza out of the oven as we walked into the kitchen.

"There's three more in there, and I can keep them coming," he said.

I thanked him as I helped the others get food first, grateful people knew us well and helped us out.

"I'll do what I can in this coming fight, but I won't deny I prefer being in here making sure you're all well fed," Holfin said as he poured us drinks. Sen got a saucer of water to dip her feet into.

"Feeding an army of elves so they can regenerate their powers and fight some more is a role in battle you can give yourself credit for," Daisy said as she walked in. She carried a crate of dart guns and ammo and pulled one out to hand Holfin. "Just in case they get this far."

Holfin didn't look pleased about being handed a weapon, but he nodded and looked at Daisy.

"I can't let any of them stop the food from flowing, now can I?" he asked.

Daisy chuckled and kissed him before grabbing a slice

of pizza and heading out to distribute the weapons to the rest of the mythicals and the others in the building who didn't have a superpower.

It was hard to relax, knowing a fight could start at any moment, but the pizzas kept coming, and as they did, different folks from the building kept popping in and out. Some of them were too nervous to want to eat much, but I welcomed them anyway. Sen or Roth soon had them feeling relaxed, getting up to their usual antics.

Most of the elves stuffed their faces along with Zephyr and me, and it made me wonder what the food bill for the building was. Thankfully the organization had recently stepped up its funding, giving the warehouse a special license and status as an elven refuge and a place of training.

We had three Shishous here when Minsheng and Jinti were around, Daisy having been promoted. I'd been bumped to leadership level as well, the training I was doing recognized. Between that and the money the dojo made, the bills were covered and then some, but it was nothing short of crazy.

By the time the pizza delivery slowed, I was stuffed, and most of the elves had gone to bed. Holfin had retired to get some shut-eye. Emily had taken over, thankfully back to help us out.

You should sleep as well, Zephyr said, getting up from the spot he'd been occupying while he stuffed his face.

I wasn't going to argue, but I wanted to check the perimeter one last time.

With Roth and Sen tucked up somewhere to sleep, I walked to the roof with Zephyr again. The stars were out and I stared at them, wishing our lives were simpler before reminding myself that I had a job to do.

Reaching out with my mind, I checked the foundations and the building one last time. Everything was still where it needed to be and as ready as we could make it.

I spread out from there, feeling the air and earth for signs of control or the presence of an obvious elf. There were still people going about their lives in LA, and I could feel them moving around, but none of them posed a threat, and none were trying to come any closer.

Despite how late it was, there were more than a few people, and it drained me. I needed to sleep and recuperate some more. There was no threat to us right now.

I'll keep watch, Zephyr said when I walked away, then looked back to see if he was coming.

You should rest too.

I don't need sleep as often as you do, and this way, I can make sure you know sooner than anyone else.

Although it was sound logic, part of me wanted to refuse and stick by his side. However, he was right. He didn't need the sleep, but I did, which meant I had to let him have his way.

I went back to Roth and Sen. They were fast asleep, and I curled up on the bed near them. It was strange not having Zephyr here with me, but it wasn't the first time he'd been away from my side since we'd bonded.

No matter how I tried, though, I couldn't sleep. I tossed and turned, imagining every noise was the beginning of an attack until I couldn't cope any longer. As the sun rose, I got up, having barely done more than doze.

Roth and Sen were still sleeping, so I left them to it. I

made my way to the roof, where I could feel Zephyr. The morning air had a chill to it, but I felt warmer as I approached Zephyr. He turned to look at me as I walked up to his flank.

Sleep didn't come easily, did it? he asked.

No. It never does before something big. And I didn't like not having you there.

He sighed and moved his tail, bringing it around me as I reached his shoulder. I leaned into him, enjoying the warmth of his body and the coziness of being wrapped up by him. It wasn't the same as a hug, but it sure felt like one.

I almost suggested you come up sooner, he added a moment later.

Maybe I should have, but I'm here now. We'll wait it out together. Doze as well. I'll keep watch for a while.

As long as you stay where you are.

I grinned, not intending to move anywhere. I loved being close to him, and I could think of no better way to await the battle that could come at any moment.

It was always the same with Zephyr. We were comfortable with each other, completely seen and known. We couldn't have kept secrets from each other if we'd wanted to, but more than that, we respected and trusted each other with everything. No matter what happened, we were in everything together—our imperfect everything bound to each other for life.

I nestled into him, appreciating the familiarity while my mind gently reached around, feeling for people approaching. The city was quieter now, the early hours of the morning when the late-nighters were heading to bed and the early risers were still considering their day and getting their clothes on.

It was peaceful and almost magical as everyone slept around me except for a couple of the gnomes we'd rescued in our earliest time as a refuge for mythicals. I could feel them moving around downstairs, patrolling and checking the perimeter.

Zephyr drifted into sleep, but from beside him, I could feel the underlying apprehension in his mind too. Sleeping while a battle was coming was one of the hardest things to do.

I tried not to add any extra thoughts and worries to his mind, knowing that while I was this close, he'd pick up on my emotions too. Instead, I sent calming thoughts his way. He slowly drifted deeper, and the sky brightened.

Some of my apprehension went with the fading night. Cherisse had never attacked during the day, and it made me feel more secure and as if we might get through this.

Another few minutes passed as the sun showed its face on the horizon, lighting the rooftop in an orange hue. It was beautiful and the fire salamanders soon came up onto the roof, nestling into their sandpit to bask in the morning light.

For a couple of minutes I enjoyed watching them, but then I felt movement from one side of the building. I concentrated my powers in that direction to feel what was happening

It didn't take me long to work out that it was the hurried movement of several elves as they came closer.

Wake up, I said before I rushed to the door.

"They're here," I called down the stairs loud enough that

Holfin could hear me. He came awake as Zephyr got to his feet.

I rushed to his side and called to Sen and Roth. Within seconds, Zephyr and I were in the air, my mind reaching for control of the building until the other elves could arrive.

I felt the attack of the nearby elves. I didn't know how many there were, but I kept my focus on my control as Zephyr rose above me, trying to work out what we were up against.

I had to concentrate as the attack increased, powerful earth elves trying to breach the walls and get into the building however they could. As Zephyr started counting numbers and identifying any elves we recognized, the rest of our forces woke up and came to the roof or stationed themselves at weaker points such as doors and windows.

The speed impressed me, and I grinned as I let the elves I was with control more of the building, freeing me up for what I did best: hurling the elements at my enemies.

I flew higher, catching up with Zephyr as he exhaled ahead of us. Grabbing the gas cloud, I moved it to the nearest group of attackers and engulfed them in it, leaving the defense of the building to everyone else.

Zephyr then flew down and picked up more elves, grabbing them with his claws and carrying them out of range. I grinned as they squealed, not having expected it. Given we were being attacked by elves who knew us, I was surprised our joint attack had started so well: six elves knocked out and another two being carried off by my dragon.

Roth and Sen joined us, the pegasus blocking a water

blast as Sen lifted darts in her little hands and ran partway down the wall, the rock hewn so her root-like feet could find purchase.

Picking more elves, I blasted one off her feet as she noticed Sen and tried to hit the myconid with something. More attacks came my way as I hovered above the edge of the building, using the air to keep me in the sky so I could see the attackers.

I was blasted with air, but I managed to adjust myself and keep my balance. I didn't mind drawing the attacks, but I needed to make sure I could continue fighting. Everyone else would defend for now.

Somewhere below, Daisy was calling the police. We'd have reinforcements from the LAPD within minutes. Then we could do more.

Before I could recover fully, one of the air elves pushed Zephyr's gas away, making sure I couldn't use it on any more of them. It was irritating but not the end of the world, since the marksmen inside the warehouse finally opened fire.

Darts flew, hitting several elves and forcing the rest to break off and retreat to cover. In the background, I could hear people screaming and making a fuss. I could only hope that innocent civilians weren't getting caught up in this as I helped guide one of Sen's darts into the leg of another elf.

Two more went down over the next few minutes. I was hit again, and I noticed that an elf was concentrating hard on one corner of the building. One of the attackers had managed to wrest control from our defenders and was trying to crumble the wall. It shook the building hard before I could reach out and hit back.

The elf reeled as I quickly tried to repair the damage and rebuild it. A moment later, one of my elves reached out to take control again. I relinquished it as I grabbed the air in front and blasted the elf that had stumbled back. Someone tried to block the air attack, but most of it got through.

Over the next few minutes, no one got anywhere, both us and them working together more effectively and blocking and defending everything launched at us. Then the cops arrived, large vans pulling up and spitting out armored men and women with gas masks, special shields, and dart guns to help us.

I grinned at the wide-eyed looks our attackers shot at them. Zephyr finally came back, having been taking elves as far away as he dared before coming back for more. He swooped down, grabbed another pair, and dropped them in the center of the police barricade that was forming.

They were quickly sedated and carried into a special vehicle to be taken to a more secure facility. I used some of the plants at the base of the building to reach toward the elves as well, finding it harder to hit them with air since they were being cautious.

I could feel them growing plants as well, but in LA, with all the concrete and buildings, it wasn't easy to grow anything. For the moment, no one could get close enough to plant them in the ground around the building. The vines I controlled, however, were easily grown and shaped, the roots deep in deliberately designed earthen beds.

Landing on the edge of the roof so I could concentrate,

I pushed the plants out and along the ground as swiftly as I could. They grew faster than anything I'd controlled before, and I managed to wrap them around three elves before one of them tried to take control.

The assault was hard, and I lost control of one vine as I wrapped the other two around the elves and lifted them into the air. At the same time, I spun them so they couldn't see the building since it would make it harder for them to attack.

I didn't have to worry about them for long, however. After the vines lifted them and held them in place, the cops quickly hit them with darts and took care of the problem.

It was effective, and combined with Zephyr grabbing elves when he could, Roth blocking the air and water attacks that came my way, Sen flinging darts with her bare hands, the cops and other non-elemental mythicals shooting from every available spot, and my capabilities, we were turning the tide of this battle.

"Surrender," I yelled. "And all of you will be shown mercy and allowed to find somewhere else to live other than the cult that has persuaded you I'm an enemy."

It wasn't a great speech, but it clearly had an impact. Several of the elves wavered and looked at each other.

When we'd heard that there were going to be attacks on all three of the main sites I was involved in protecting, I had panicked, but I looked at the array of elves and how many defenders we had and knew this battle was as good as won.

CHAPTER TWENTY-ONE

None of the elves surrendered and we had fought on, trading blows and expending energy to prove that we were far stronger. Slowly the advantage had tipped toward us, however.

As more elves were knocked out by Zephyr's breath weapon, ran out of power, or were hit with darts, I found myself wondering what was going on. This was easy. None of the elves had come close to getting past our defenses. It was almost as if we were facing the worst elves from the mountain.

Were we?

If we were, that might mean bad things for everyone else.

But well over two hours had passed since the battle had begun, and the elves that were left fought on with everything they had. All of them did. None of them gave up, no matter what I shouted from the ramparts.

Something wasn't right about this battle.

We're being distracted. They're trying to keep us fighting for as long as possible, knowing they were never supposed to win, Zephyr said, confirming my suspicions.

How do you want to handle it?

We've almost finished them. Back off and go find Ronan's communication stone. We'll handle the rest.

Are you sure?

Entirely, he replied as he swooped. Instead of grabbing the elves as they ducked, he exhaled gas over four of them. All of them were knocked out in seconds; then the LAPD swarmed the location, their gas masks ensuring they could do so safely.

I watched for a few more seconds, using the air to blast one more elf off their feet before I jumped from the wall onto the roof and sprinted for the door inside.

The communication stone was where I always kept it when not in use, inside a small pocket in my ready bag. For a while, we'd considered not keeping a ready bag after the world had finally calmed down about having mythicals in it, but I was glad we'd continued. It was needed because the elves were fighting other elves.

I quickly reached in and pulled it out, finding it warm. It sucked me in, and I stood before Ronan and Gwaelon. It appeared as if they'd been talking, and I got the impression that I had interrupted them mid-flow.

"Aella. It is good to hear from you," Ronan said as he bowed.

"The warehouse is under attack, but we have it under control. How is the Sanctuary?" I asked, bowing back and not missing a beat.

"It is safe. We have dealt with the majority of the attack

directed at us. It was...easy. Thankfully, Gwaelon thinks he may know the reason."

"I think they're all distractions," the elf said, looking at me.

"It would seem that way. Do you know what it's a distraction from?" I asked, although I suspected.

"The portal here in Mexico. They're gearing up to break through," Gwaelon said. "But they're not ready yet. They need something they don't have."

I frowned, but I thought I knew what they needed— that tablet Minsheng had. I said as much.

"It's possible it's that, but..." It was Ronan's turn to look serious.

"What?" I asked, feeling the urgency in working out what they were after.

"Those tablets were rarely kept alone. Often a teacher who used them would have an entire stash of similar devices, some to help boost an elf's powers as well. It's why the Sanctuary is so driven to know how they came to find the tablet."

I exhaled, not sure whether to be angry that Ronan hadn't told me, angry the government was hiding the information, or sad that no one seemed to trust me with everything when I was trying to keep everyone safe. Now wasn't the time for any of those emotions, however.

There was nothing to be done but contact Minsheng and, if needed, rush to the portal site in Texas. I had to hope that I could get there in time if they were in the trouble I thought they were.

"I'll do what I can and keep the stone on me from now on. Keep me informed as you can. I'll assume the Sanctuary is safe for now and that the Mexico portal is the target," I said as I pulled back mentally, hoping Ronan would let me out of the dark headspace.

Slowly the room I was in came back into view. For a couple of seconds, I stayed where I was, not sure how to process everything I had been told.

Is everything okay? Zephyr asked.

I could feel him and my other mythicals on the roof and in the sky, no doubt doing as they offered. As I followed the connections with my mind, I thought about the best way to explain what Ronan and Gwaelon had said and what it might mean. Zephyr was quiet when I finished speaking, his emotions troubled.

We need to find out what's going on, Zephyr said eventually. *Tell the President if he doesn't let us know exactly what they found, I plan to eat him for lunch.*

I laughed, unable to contain it. Zephyr sounded serious enough that it made me wonder, but I planned to pass the message on as deadpan as Zephyr had told me.

Finding my phone, I called my Shishou. It rang for long enough that I panicked that something had happened to Minsheng and I wasn't going to get through to him.

"Aella?" he said, finally picking up. "Now isn't a great time. We're under attack."

"I know. We've been hit too, as has the Sanctuary. But we've clearly gotten the bluff. I take it you haven't?"

"We're struggling," Minsheng replied.

I heard a grunt and weapons firing. I tried to stay calm, but I wanted to scream my Shishou's name and demand he tell me he was okay.

"They seem to be trying to get into something else,

though. Almost as if they don't want the portal," Minsheng finally said, confirming that he was okay.

"They don't. I think the President and the military haven't told us everything. They found something else with the tablet, and that's what Cherisse sent her elves to get."

I waited for a response since there was the sound of another small scuffle in the background. It was hard to listen and wait, but I could hear Minsheng's breathing this time and could tell he was still alive.

"I wouldn't be surprised if you're right, but I don't think they're likely to tell me."

"No. They're not. But they will tell me. I want to talk to the President as soon as is humanly possible."

"That's not going to be easy. I'm not sure where he is. I think he was whisked to an underground bunker. But I'll do what I can. I'll get back to you." With that, Minsheng hung up, and I was once again holding a communication device that wouldn't do any more.

Sighing and feeling so many things, I grabbed my pack. It was time to go back to Texas and as quickly as possible.

I made my way up to the roof, passing Daisy as I did.

"They need you at one of the other places?" she asked.

I nodded, not sure how to explain when I felt so mixed about it.

"We've got this. The LAPD made a huge difference with the equipment and tactics you suggested to them," Daisy said. "Go make sure my brother comes back in one piece."

"Always," I replied, hoping I could. It sounded as if he were in trouble, and I still had to get there.

By the time I was on the roof, there was a message on my phone.

There is a plane waiting for you at the nearest airport. It can bring you here just as fast and save you the energy. We need you.

It was from Minsheng, and I knew it was an understatement. It was a relief, however. I wanted to be where I could help most, and having the US military get me where I needed to be was a good sign that the right people realized they needed me.

Zephyr was high in the air, but I called to Sen, and the dryad came running up the wall as I approached. Roth flew past me as I scooped her up and tucked her into my jacket. She beamed at me, another dart in her hand and a mischievous look in her eyes. I was pretty sure she had at least one attack in mind.

As I launched, an elf came out of nowhere, also flying, albeit not as steadily as I was. I swerved around him, feeling him try to take control of the air holding me up. Before I could attempt to return the favor, Sen reached out of the top of my jacket and threw the dart she was carrying at him.

It stuck fast, and his mind began shutting down. I used my ability to steady him, then eased him onto the roof. Someone could take care of him later.

Although it felt wrong to be leaving my home partway through a battle, I knew everyone was doing an amazing job. In the time I had been talking to the other locations and checking in with them, more Amcika elves had been taken out, and the warehouse was safer. They didn't need me anymore, and hopefully, they'd cope without Sen, Roth, and Zephyr for a while.

It would have been easier if we'd been able to sneak out, but I was sure the elves would know we were coming long before we arrived as it was.

Zephyr flew ahead, scanning the area and making sure the elves didn't have a surprise for us in case we or others at the warehouse had to flee.

Of course, there wasn't much we could do about it if there was. I needed to get to the portal, and there wasn't much variation on the route. There wasn't time.

Waiting at the airport in LA was the familiar large cargo plane. Zephyr landed first, making it clear he planned to go inside, no questions asked.

I hurried after him and hoped Roth would soon catch up. He struggled to fly as fast as Zephyr and I could, but he didn't seem to mind struggling behind us. I felt guilty about that, but we needed to get to Texas, and we couldn't burn out my power to do so swiftly.

As soon as Roth touched down and galloped up the ramp, the cargo plane moved forward, the back shutting as it taxied down the runway. I found somewhere to sit as I pulled out my phone and let Minsheng know we were on the way to him.

I tried not to worry, but there was something about this entire day I was struggling to comprehend. It felt crazy to divide us like this and throw away her elves unless something bigger was happening. I knew opening a portal was the important thing for Cherisse, but this wasn't attempting any of those things.

Just as I was thinking that, I received another message from Minsheng.

They've pinned us down. We can hold for a while, but we're going to run out of ammo and the elves are going to run out of power before they'll give up.
I'm coming as fast as I can.

I tapped out my response as quickly as I could and put the phone somewhere I'd notice it before getting to my feet again. I needed to hurry things up, and that meant going to see the pilot.

The soldiers on board the plane with us weren't enthusiastic about letting me go toward the pilot, but I glared at anyone who tried to stop me or get in my way. They backed off and let me go to the cockpit.

Once there, I explained to the pilot that I wanted to make the plane fly faster and asked about that. He frowned, clearly not convinced I could, but I wouldn't let him turn me away. I lingered, my mind reaching over the plane, getting a feel for how it worked and the way the air flowed over it.

While he flew, I made a few tweaks and aided the plane. I wasn't sure how much difference it made until I realized that the co-pilot had turned and was looking between me and one of the panels on the large dashboard in front of them.

"It's working," he said.

I grinned and kept going.

Be careful, Zephyr cautioned. *Remember that we are going to need your power when we get there.*

Good point, I replied before looking for the nearest soldier.

"Is there any food aboard?" I asked as soon as I saw another person.

They lifted their eyebrows but went off to look, and I turned my attention back to the plane. We were going to get to Texas as soon as I could manage it. With any luck, it would be soon enough.

CHAPTER TWENTY-TWO

Two hours later, I was exhausted and forced to eat again.

I was pretty sure the soldiers on board had ransacked every cupboard and personal bag or cargo crate on the plane and brought me all the food. Part of me felt guilty, but this was how I refueled, and I couldn't continue any other way.

I sat myself down near Zephyr's head and leaned against his shoulder. I could feel the concern emanating from him without looking at him, and again I felt guilty. I knew he was relying on me to make sensible decisions. They all were.

Rest, Zephyr said. *We're all doing our best. We have a lot of hard decisions to make right now. A lot of people need all of us. We're part of a team, and it will be none of our faults if we don't succeed.*

I exhaled before taking another bite. Someone had found some old crackers, all that was left. They weren't particularly appetizing, but food was food.

Feeling my eyes begin to close, I leaned against Zephyr.

His tail swept up and around me, thankfully not knocking anyone over in the tight space as he did so.

I wasn't sure if I should be fighting the tiredness, but I couldn't have if I'd wanted to. After not sleeping the night before and fighting for a lot of the morning, I didn't have much left in me.

Zephyr moving stirred me, but I had no idea how much time had passed.

We're here, he said, his head nuzzling into me. That passed as a hug while he was in dragon form.

I got to my feet, still groggy but feeling better for having eaten and slept. The plane hadn't landed yet, but I could see the runway and the buildings that had been erected around the portal cavern that formed the base. It was quiet. Too quiet. Fear filled me.

There haven't been any messages from Minsheng, Zephyr pointed out. *I'm sure if the elves had gotten through and anything had happened to him, we'd know about it.*

Although I wanted to be reassured by Zephyr, and I was pretty sure he was right, I still felt apprehensive and rushed to the back of the plane to wait by the hatch. As soon as it was open wide enough, I powered through the gap, aiming for the ground beside it.

I was grateful to see soldiers rushing over, some bringing equipment and fuel tanks to service the plane. It didn't take me long to spot the major. He was sporting a fresh wound on one arm, but it had been bandaged. He looked like his usual cheery self, if tired around the eyes.

"What happened?" I asked as I felt rather than saw Roth and Zephyr get off the plane to come to my side.

"We've managed to resecure the base. And the portal is safe," the major said a moment later.

"And Minsheng?"

"Also safe. He was hurt, but the doctor is seeing to him, and he'll be fine. A broken bone, I think, but no worse."

I frowned, not sure I liked the sound of that, but Seth came up to me. His clothes were singed, but he also appeared to be in good health.

"Well, that was chaos. We could have done with you here, Henera," he said, the last word surprising me.

"I came as quickly as I could. The Sanctuary made it through, and I think the warehouse did too. I left before the battle had finished when I realized the real target was here."

Seth blinked and the major let out a whistle, then ran a hand through his hair.

"You were willing to leave your own home and the people locked in battle to try to get here in time to help us?" Seth asked.

I nodded. "I won't deny that I left them in a good state. The battle was all but over, but it hadn't finished."

"And she did everything she could to get the plane to fly faster as well," the pilot said as he disembarked. "Jack is saying she's likely to be heading back out as soon as she's ready again, though."

The major nodded, wincing. I had a feeling there was more for me to learn.

"You want to fly me somewhere else?" I asked.

"Possibly, but I think you probably ought to come see the colonel and Minsheng before anything is set in stone. They know more and can probably explain what happened here better. I was stuck in the portal room most of the time, and I don't know everything."

While it frustrated me that I wasn't being told all that was known, I appreciated that the major was trying to get me the most information the soonest and was treating me with respect. Zephyr nudged me encouragingly to follow him. Roth fell in beside me with Sen on his back, clutching his mane so she didn't fall off as he moved.

I let the major lead me to the main building, and I saw the damage. The front of the building was warped, twisted as if someone had tried to pry it off with a massive can opener.

Two earth elementals were standing by it, slowly fixing it and trying to keep it stable as they reattached parts. Had it been a normal day, I'd have stopped to help them, but if I was being sent somewhere else, I wouldn't have the capacity or power to do so. I made a mental note to let the Sanctuary know if I could.

There was a chance the large city had enough that they could spare an earth elf or possibly two. And if not, the warehouse had fared well enough that they could help.

I didn't get to think about it anymore, however, as I walked into the building and saw the carnage inside. If the front looked bad, the interior was worse. It was scorched in places and drenched in others. Fearing to go farther but knowing I needed to, I kept walking, treading carefully and hoping Roth and Zephyr could get through.

Eventually, I spotted Minsheng sitting on the edge of a broken desk with a medic putting a splint on his leg and checking it was holding his limb straight.

As I went to him, I tried not to look shocked. Despite

the pain he must have been in, he smiled the moment he saw me.

"You made it. We didn't hold on until you got here, but we did our best. Sorry, Aella. You're going to have to go stop them, and you're going to need as much help as you can get."

"Tell me everything," I said, sitting down on a nearby half-broken chair.

Minsheng looked thoughtful.

"It was a strange attack, as if they were trying to outnumber us swiftly. They definitely meant us to be overwhelmed, and most of their forces were aimed here. We rushed to defend the portal, thinking that was why they were here. But they weren't, and we realized too late to defend it properly."

"You did your best. We were all fooled," I replied, hearing the sorrow in his voice.

"They took the tablet and my research."

"Yeah. That's what I expected when I spoke to you on the phone. It is done, but I need to go after them."

"I was hoping you would say that," came a voice from behind.

I turned to see the President, his suit dusty. The security personnel with him were on edge.

It was unexpected, and I almost asked what he'd been doing on the site when we knew the attack was coming.

"Do you know where I need to go?" I asked instead.

"It would appear you need to head to Mexico," he replied. "I've been talking to the ambassador there. You're clear to enter the country and act as you see fit. It sounds as if you're going to have a mountain of elves to deal with."

I thought of Gwaelon and how convinced he had been that something would be happening elsewhere. It wasn't a good indicator that he was okay, and I wasn't sure I was all right with everything. The Mexican mountain was a crazy place to be heading into.

Had this been what they wanted? To lure us into their domain once more? Ronan had pointed out that I would defend my home better. Did Cherisse know that her elves were the same?

I had to take several deep breaths as panic and my memories of my last time in the place threatened to over-whelm me. I didn't want to go there again, but I couldn't sit back and wait for them to open the portal. I had to go to Mexico.

We should take all the backup we can get, Zephyr said. *If this is truly their plan, we don't need to defend the portal here, the Sanctuary, or the warehouse.*

Are you sure?

We can't do it alone. Not against an entire mountain full of well-trained elves. Not even Gwaelon being on the inside will give us enough of an advantage. We're going to be laying siege to it and breaking in, all before they attempt to open the portal.

I'm not sure I can ask anyone to come with us and face that place. A shudder rippled through me.

There will be plenty of volunteers. No one wants those portals open. They're going to destroy us all if they're not careful.

It was all the encouragement I needed.

"We're going to need to pick up more mythicals and supplies," I said. "Is there time for that?"

"We'll make time," the President replied. "Who and what do you need?"

I thought for a second, but before I could get up, several soldiers stepped forward, and elves with them.

"We'll come with you," the one in front said. "We've gotten some unfinished business, and there's no way we're letting them get away with taking something that's ours."

As I acknowledged their offer, I was pretty sure I heard Zephyr let out a low chuckle. So far, it was going pretty much how he said it would, and I knew that would be funny to him.

I didn't have to look any farther to see more volunteers step up. The President ushered everyone into a bigger space, and soldiers rushed around, trying to get us organized. Minsheng found a metal pole he could use as a crutch, but I held my hand up.

"You're hurt," I said.

"And we both know that mythicals heal more quickly than others," he replied. "Besides, I don't need to wade into battle. But you might need my information, and I can't watch you go into danger once more without doing everything I can to help."

There was no arguing with that logic, and if it was me, I'd feel the same. With that decided, I made my way to where everyone was gathering. I noticed there were a lot of elves and soldiers and yet more who were bringing ammo, supplies, and food.

I grabbed an energy bar and munched as I tried to get the measure of who I was going to have with me, then I went to my pack and pulled out my communication stone.

I need privacy. And I'll need you to stay in the real world this time, I said to Zephyr. I would have gone and found a room, but it was clear there weren't many that were safe.

223

Without hesitation, Zephyr moved his body and unfolded one wing, bringing it up and over me.

I sat against him, and Roth came over to block the angle Zephyr couldn't. Grateful for them, I used the stone to reach out to Ronan, slipping into the dark room his mind would be connected to.

It took him a moment to appear, and he noticed I was alone.

"I can't take too long, but you should know what's been happening. The elves hit the portal site. They've not opened the portal, but they've taken the tablet. We're going to need to follow them to Mexico, or they're going to open that portal instead."

Ronan blinked, trying to take in everything I'd said.

"You're going to assault the mountain," he replied.

I nodded.

"Are you coming here on the way?"

"I was planning to."

"We'll be ready. As many of us as possible." Ronan nodded at me, his respect and conviction making me want to cry with relief.

"Only volunteers."

"They'll happily do so."

I exhaled as I disconnected, then reached for my phone as Zephyr and Roth moved to let me up. I tapped out a message to Daisy saying something similar to Ronan, then I grabbed another energy bar.

"Time to go," I said. "Sanctuary, then the airport near LA, and then Mexico."

The President nodded, but he didn't need to speak. The major had everyone move out to the plane we'd come in on. As soon as I got out there, I noticed it was still being checked and plenty of people were loading the back of it.

"We've gotten another plane flying in to join you and carry the rest of the troops and anyone else who volunteers," the major said as he fell in beside me.

"Good. I need to rest, but I want to know before we land anywhere to pick people up. I want to greet them and make sure I know who I've gotten and what they're capable of."

"Yes, ma'am. I'll see you know what you need to." The major winked, making me laugh as Zephyr, Roth, Sen, and I made our way into the large cargo plane.

It was more cramped inside now, more than a few others coming with us, along with the ammunition and cargo needed for them to fight.

Are you going to be okay? I asked Zephyr as he shifted his weight and almost crushed a stack of food crates.

For a short journey, he replied, but I could hear discomfort in his voice.

I used my wind powers to lift and move some crates to make the gap more him-shaped. He relaxed, but it still wasn't perfect.

Thankfully, there was little more to do to get the plane ready to fly again. We were soon in the air, surrounded by elves, soldiers, and mythicals ready to stop Cherisse before it was too late.

CHAPTER TWENTY-THREE

I could barely think. Before me stood an army of mythicals and soldiers. Everyone at the warehouse had secured the building and made their way to the Sanctuary while we flew there. I stood before them all.

In the past, we'd had volunteers to go into battle, especially in the elven community and the centaurs, but this time, the soldiers were standing alongside them. There were also dwarves and gnomes and so many mythical creatures it felt as if we had a small zoo with us.

"I want you all to know that what you're offering to do with me today is not small. You are all being brave beyond anything that could be expected of you. You have my respect, every one of you, and you have my promise that I'll stand by you in battle. We'll do this together. All of us. United."

There was a cheer as I stepped forward, and without thinking about what I was doing, I led my mythicals into the group to stand with them.

"Aella. Henera!" someone cried from my left.

I tried to turn to see who it had been, but more people took up the chant until I was in the middle of an excited mob calling for me to lead them into battle.

Fear crept through me as I thought about how some of them could die. Each situation we walked into was more dangerous than the last, but I had to push past that. I didn't have time for doubt. If I froze in indecision, I would get someone killed.

We'll do our best and know it's enough, Zephyr said. *We've trained for this, and they know it. We'll honor them.*

With Zephyr's calming words and the belief he had in our small team washing over me, I lifted my head and raised my arm.

"Together," I yelled, unable to speak my name or the elven nickname I'd been given.

They took up the word, adding it to their cries until we were all chanting and making our way onto the aircraft that stood before us. The major helped organize everyone, the majority of the mythical creatures going on another cargo-style plane while everyone in a humanoid form was ushered onto a passenger-style aircraft.

I followed Zephyr again, thinking about the best plan of action when it came to attacking the mountain and getting to the portal as quickly as possible. We had a lot more support than I'd expected with the group that had come to help rescue me with Minsheng when we'd been trapped in the mountain.

But getting us out hadn't needed as many elves. I'd been able to get myself most of the way, and I'd then had to punch through and flee. We had not needed to fight most of the elves living in the mountain.

This time we would have to fight our way through them, and there were a lot. On top of that, they were defending what they believed in and a place they called home. That would give them an advantage.

As soon as the plane was in the air, I sat down with Minsheng, Ronan, the major, Vestan, Seth, and my mythicals to make a plan. It wasn't going to be easy, but we were going to give ourselves the best advantage we could.

It took a long time, all of us eating while we flew and talked. Sometimes the conversation grew heated as one person thought of something another hadn't, but eventually, we were in agreement. We knew what we were doing and who we were doing it with.

There was a strong mix of types of support, from soldiers and humanoids with traditional weaponry to elementals and mythicals with what would have once been called a superpower. With any luck, they would help us stop a portal from being opened before the end of the day.

"I am worried about Gwaelon," Ronan said as others left the group to issue the commands.

"You're not the only one," I replied.

"It would appear the elves deliberately gave him false information, and it might cost us everything."

"It hasn't yet, but it makes me worry for him nonetheless. I will make it a priority to find him."

"No. He wouldn't want that," Ronan said, although I saw the sadness in his eyes. "If we saved him but the portal was opened, he would have to carry that guilt for the rest of his life. Sometimes we have to make the tough decisions, as Lorcan did."

I nodded, unable to speak as I was reminded of the

death of the great centaur. It had been him giving his life for something. For me. I carried some guilt and always would.

But more than one person had reassured me that it was what he would have wanted, and I knew what mattered most was making a difference. With that in mind, I made my way to the small area by Zephyr I could rest in.

I was going to make sure I had every inch of power I possessed. If this battle went the way I thought, I was going to be running on empty by the end.

When we were only twenty minutes out, I got up, ate some more, and went over the plan with each group's leader one last time.

Finally, I was as ready as I was ever going to be, and the plane was landing. There were still groups of people on the other planes who didn't know what was going to be needed of them, and we were still a few miles north of the mountain.

Thankfully, the government of the US had worked with the Mexican government, and we would have transport to take us to the mountain's base. We tell everyone else what they would be doing along the way.

It did mean Amcika would see us coming, however. There were too many of us and it was still daytime. But we would hit them hard and fast and hope we made it.

The weakest part of our plan was hoping the staircase we'd hidden in still existed and that we could get to it. If it didn't, we were all going to have to use the elevator shaft. We weren't likely to get enough elves up the inside of the mountain fast enough with that alone. It was too narrow and too easily controlled by a few air elves.

With nothing I could do to change that part of the plan and no better alternative, I hurried off the plane beside Zephyr. Sen had tucked herself into my jacket. Although I was going to be mostly using my elemental powers, I had a large dart gun strapped to my leg and ammo in my pockets, vying for space with food.

One of the gnomes at the Sanctuary had given Sen her very own weapon, a blowgun that allowed her to shoot her little darts at an incredible range. Roth had not been ignored either, the pegasus adorned with a water weapon that would allow him to store the water he absorbed and aim it at his attackers with better precision.

Roth was delighted with it, and I knew it was likely to come in handy. On top of that, we'd filled it full of water for him. He was going to be a massive asset in battle.

I gathered all the air elves, along with any mythicals who could fly. We would climb the mountain fastest and try to secure the portal, so I needed as many as possible. It helped that I knew the air capabilities of the mountain elves, having fought them when I was trying to escape.

Despite our backup and our plan, I didn't feel confident as everyone made their way to the transport. I didn't get into one of the large coaches but climbed onto Zephyr's back. Although we normally preserved his strength as well, there wasn't much he could do inside a mountain. As such, it made sense that he flew with me and we acted as the scouting party.

By the time he was in the air, everyone was off the planes and geared up for battle. It felt strange to be leading such a large army, and once again, the icy grip of fear tried to squeeze my heart and freeze my thoughts and body. The last time I'd been in this mountain, I had been terrified. Seeing it up ahead of us made those memories come flooding back.

We can do this, Zephyr said, his voice confident and deep. *All of us have been trained for this, and you know their secrets now.*

It was the last opportunity he got to say anything since air scouts from Cherisse's cult spotted Zephyr and me in the air. One of them rushed toward the mountain, but the other three came straight for us.

Without hesitation, I ignored the scouts closest and blasted the one trying to warn the elves inside the mountain with all the air I could. At the same time, I reached for control of the area to stop her from recovering.

It was right on the edge of my range, and my control of it was weaker than I'd have liked, but Zephyr flew us closer, his powerful wings driving us through the air.

I could feel the elves who were powering toward us trying to take control from me or blast me with air, but they didn't manage to unseat me from Zephyr's back before the elves below us noticed what was going on. Several air elves came to my rescue, blasting into the air out of the transport truck they were in.

Knowing that I could forget about the elves nearest me, I returned my attention to the scout. She had increased the distance between us, but I didn't give up and used my powers to help Zephyr propel us forward faster.

As the gap closed again, I took control of the air around the fleeing elf and blasted her downward once more. Although the mountain wasn't far away, I had an advantage and kept blasting her down and away, stealing her control.

When she was close to crashing to the ground, I paused and tried to stop her from landing hard, but I either had underestimated what I was capable of or overestimated her ability to correct. She still hit the ground with a thud that would have hurt anyone. She bounced, and I tried to cushion her.

Thankfully, she soon moved, letting me know she was alive as Zephyr flew closer and lower. I watched her until I was sure she wasn't a threat anymore, then returned my attention to the elves behind us.

They had been dealt with as well and I exhaled, relief flooding through me at having managed to get this far without letting any scouts get back to the mountain and warn Cherisse we were coming. I noted that it had lost us time as the air elves who had come to my defense flew back down to rejoin the others.

It was often the way in battle that you had to decide in the heat of the moment if something was worth doing. I had no idea if the scout getting back to the mountain would have made the impending battle a lot harder, and I had no way to know if we should have preserved the energy we had used.

All I could do was try my best, as I'd been told many times.

We reached the mountain quickly. It loomed tall and imposing by the time the first transport came to a halt, at the end of its usefulness.

Knowing it wouldn't be hard for the elves to know we were coming, Zephyr circled down and preserved his energy for the coming fight.

The soldiers were the first to get out of the vehicles and

into something resembling a formation, their years of practice and training making them far more efficient than my elves.

The Sanctuary elves were next, most of them having trained with the elven masters for some time. They were quick to get into familiar groups. I knew all of them had benefited from the best training going, but I also knew they weren't fighters. At least, they hadn't been trained to be, given the methods the masters had always used.

Of course, my presence in the Sanctuary's everyday life had changed that a little.

The warehouse elves made up the last bunch. They were also the smallest group, but I looked them over and noted with satisfaction that they were also some of the strongest elves I knew. In a fight, they were all useful in their own way, but we would find out if we had what we needed as one large army.

As we approached the main entrance to the mountain, it opened. Cherisse stepped out as Zephyr landed, bridging the gap between my army and hers.

"Have you finally come to your senses?" Cherisse asked. "Or is this pathetic rabble here to attempt something foolish?"

"Hand us back what you stole," I declared as I slid off Zephyr's back to stand beside him.

Cherisse laughed, and I was not surprised by her reaction. I'd not expected anything else, but it was the right thing to offer her an alternative.

"Go back to your Sanctuary and your stupid warehouse in LA and leave me to my work."

"I can't. You're not opening that portal, not when I

know evil lurks on the other side," I replied, knowing it would make little difference.

"You can't stop us from opening the portal. This is my last warning. Go, or be escorted off this mountain with force."

I rolled my eyes at the drama and lifted a fist into the air, not uttering a word as it triggered our attack. Everyone with a gun opened fire and Cherisse's eyes went wide.

Enjoying having the upper hand if for only a moment, I reached out and took control of the elements. It was time to begin this fight.

CHAPTER TWENTY-FOUR

The fight was chaos. There were so many darts flying through the air, so much water vapor and rain, fires starting, and rocks and plants moving that shouldn't be that I lifted into the air above the battlefield to try to make sense of it all.

The soldiers had tilted the battle in our favor at the start, and more than a few elves lay where they had fallen, feathered projectiles sticking out of their chests. But the elves of the mountain were defending their home, and they were giving our elves a run for their money.

We needed to push Cherisse back so we could get into the building and start working our way up to the portal, although it filled me with great dread to think about being inside again.

She's got a weak spot, Zephyr said, circling above me.

I dodged a blast of air from a cultist several hundred yards below me as I tried to spot what he meant.

By the left-hand side of the entrance? I asked after studying it a moment longer.

Where the earth elves are struggling.

I saw what Zephyr was talking about. There were four earth elves using plants to try to block an area of the entrance and narrow the gap Cherisse and the elves with her had to defend.

I watched as some of the Sanctuary earth elves tried to take control and didn't succeed. Yet despite the Sanctuary elves not being a threat, something or someone was making the plants grow in strange directions.

While the plants continued to thrash about, I scanned the crowds of moving people, looking for whoever it could be.

Sen do it, the myconid said, lifting her head above the collar of my jacket.

I paused, not sure how that was possible. Was Sen controlling the plants?

There was no way to test it. I was inclined to believe her, but I was still shocked. This wasn't a phenomenon I'd ever heard of happening. It wasn't a surprise that Zephyr could use my powers in human form. He was a dragon descendant who had elven ancestry. Sen and Roth were significantly less likely to have been creatures who could control elementals.

Today, however, my mythicals had brought their abilities and talents to the fight, and we were working our way forward. Sen continued to put the air elves I might have to deal with later on the back foot, and I landed on the battlefield not far from them.

Sen stayed tucked up in my jacket, her body protected by me and the forces around us. Although she was wearing her tiny set of dragon scale armor and she had a prototype of a little flying device that fit her, the latter was unstable and had been created by Chris. She was safer close to me, doing what she could from the safety I could offer her.

As soon as we were on the ground, I started a spinning vortex a few feet ahead of me, catching the plants not controlled by Sen.

It was easy to get the spin and tightness right, but everything else was hard, especially getting it to grow. There wasn't a lot here to work with, but I knew I could get it larger and more effective.

I felt another air elf from the Sanctuary slip their control in near mine, helping to separate the cooler and hotter air to get the conditions right and keep it building. It spun faster and higher and pulled in more of the debris around it.

I didn't hesitate to move it toward the Amcika elves and try to suck up the plants and earth they were using to make the entrance smaller. With Sen causing them problems as well, we soon destroyed the defenses they were trying to erect and got the bonus of flinging the detritus at high speed at the defenders.

Part of me felt bad that I was hurting so many of the mountain elves, but a lot more people would be hurt if the portal was opened.

Cherisse seemed to sense the battle wasn't going well. She was slowly working her way back into the group of elves as I and everyone with me pressed forward.

Now and then, a blast of air or water or a rumble of earth almost knocked me off my feet, but I had a small team of elves who were concentrating on defending me as well as making progress. They helped keep me going and

Zephyr and Roth did the rest, blocking attacks and flying around me.

Pushing the advantage, we moved forward, blasting elves back with jets of air as I let go of the tornado. The air elves with me took control between them and used it to aid in pushing the elves into the mountain.

With Cherisse inside, the pressure broke the resistance, and they fell back into the mountain. Before they could shut the large door or do anything else to block the way, Zephyr barreled forward, his scales taking the brunt of several jets of fire and blasts of air before my elves and I could come around him and fight back.

I felt the extra difficulty since everything inside the mountain was marked by the control of the elves within it. The group wavered, caught on the boundary as we were hit with everything they had. So much air blasted at us that it was hard to hold steady.

We need the water elves to hurry up, Zephyr said, the strain in his voice making him sound as if he'd gritted his teeth.

I reached out to the stairwell opening, shielding behind him as I did. There was rock covering the opening again, and it was thicker than it had been when we'd busted out to escape the mountain. I could feel the control of some elves on the other side as they tried to work their way through it.

The movement was subtle, and we needed speed. Without hesitation, I used my mind to pull the rock apart, creating a well in the wall to my right while everyone was distracted.

Although I could feel the control of the Sanctuary earth

elves inside the tunnel I'd hidden in, I couldn't be sure they were close or ready for the opening I was giving them. However, we needed something to help us, and it was the only thing I could think of.

As Zephyr slipped back, making it impossible for any more elves to get through the opening, I broke through the wall. The earth elves in Cherisse's cult finally noticed what was happening and I felt them trying to stop me, their minds hitting mine.

It took all my concentration to keep the rocky surface under my control while peeling back layers and swiftly making the hole bigger. I felt the other elves responding, picking up the pace and adding more space to what I was doing. When the hole was large enough to admit a small car, I was suddenly alone in my work again.

Are they finally ready? Zephyr asked, the strain he was under coming out in every word.

I think so, I replied as I reached around him with my mind, trying to push the air back and form a barrier. We were about to need it. At the same time, I reached into the floor below us and lifted a rim of earth to protect us. It wouldn't help us move forward yet, but we were about to need protection from some water.

No sooner had I thought this than I felt and heard the rush of water as it poured out of the hole in the side tunnel like an overly large fire hydrant gone wrong. I directed it at the air elves pushing us back and anyone else who looked as if they were going to get in our way.

The pressure on Zephyr eased, and he took another step forward.

As water started pouring back along the floor, I stayed

where I was and raised it again to keep the deluge from rushing toward the elves coming into the mountain behind me.

More joined us as the water slowly ebbed away, the water elves responsible for it growing tired and none of us wanting so much water in the place that could be turned against us.

It meant the fire elementals were hampered, and the earth elementals were frantically trying to close the gap I'd opened up again. The moment of chaos had broken their neat ranks, however, and we continued to press the advantage, not letting any of them recover.

Roth flew down to land in the water. I felt it bring an extra burst of life and energy to him as he soaked up the water and began preparing to hit the elves with it again.

I could have laughed, but I pushed forward with Zephyr, making more room for the elves and soldiers to join us. When the major appeared, I gave him a brief nod. He would be in charge down here. I was taking some forces and heading up, but not up the way everyone expected.

Pushing elves out of the way with rock, air, or water, depending on what I could take control of more easily and snatch from the enemy, I made my way to the hole I'd made. My air elves joined me, helping me blast strategic elves off their feet along the way.

There was no sign of Cherisse now. That almost made me stop to look for her, but I kept going. There was a good chance she'd abandoned the elves down here to fight, but it could also mean she was going to attempt to open the portal. That, I couldn't allow.

We need to hurry, I told Zephyr as we continued to push forward. He was using his dragon body to charge the elves and knock them out of the way or make them run.

That hole also needs to be wider, he replied. The gap leading to the stairs was only big enough for the water stream the water elves had pushed through it. I reached for it and tried to pull the rock apart as the air elves with me and the water elves from the tunnel started moving through the gap at as high a speed as they could manage.

It wasn't easy to terraform an area that had so many people moving over and past it, but I did my best, chipping it away and making it wider. I thought about Gwaelon, who we still hadn't seen. I was more than ready to find out where he was and get him into the fight, but I was worried about him.

When I reached the hole, I moved to go through it despite it not being wide enough for Zephyr. Sen tucked herself into my jacket again, having taken a potshot at an elf with her little blowgun. Roth was standing to one side, jetting water and using his body to shield a pair of water elves as they controlled the liquid that hadn't yet managed to drain.

I focused on the wall as I went through, noticing it was a lot thicker than the last time we had been there. It was going to take a few minutes to widen it to dragon-size.

As I finally got it broad enough for Zephyr to fit through, I spotted Ruehnar. The water master looked tired but pleased with himself. I should have known he'd be behind the water attack.

"Want to come with me to find your brother?" I asked.

"You don't need to ask. I was going to insist upon it," the water master replied.

There was no way I'd have denied him, and we both knew it.

As soon as Zephyr had squeezed through the gap in the wall, his wings unfurling from where he'd pressed them against his body, we were all ready to go up.

I pulled a flashlight out of my pocket and turned it on, grateful for the US military and what they'd provided for us. All the elves who were helping with my part of things did as well until the abandoned staircase was lit up. It was only then that I realized how stunning it was and that it swept up in beautifully carved bends.

The walls had been decorated with a painted design. It was faded now, but it had once been grand and ornate. I stopped, looking at it and wishing I'd been able to appreciate it the last time I'd been in the place.

You never said how beautiful it is in here, I told Zephyr as we climbed.

I couldn't see it very well, and I spent the entire time trying to help you stay calm and guide you. I'd also been away from you for several days and out in the cold. I was focused on us and how much better it felt to have you close.

My mouth fell open as I tried to form the words for an apology and take back the snarkiness I'd asked the question with, then I felt a wave of affection come to me from Zephyr and relaxed.

We've got a job to do. It's okay. Let's stop Cherisse and make sure this portal is secure.

It was a good point, and it helped me focus. We needed

to get to the top swiftly, which meant we had to get on with it.

As a group, we made our way up, stopping now and then to feel for the control of other elves. It took a while, and as we ascended, the sounds of battle faded.

Now that I was significantly better practiced at taking control of marked elements and feeling for them, I noticed that some levels of the mountain had strongly marked elements, and on others, it had faded. Many were different, marked by another or in a strange way.

If this place hadn't been in the hands of an enemy, it would have been a useful place to study the long-term changes of elves. I had a feeling I was never going to get that kind of opportunity.

When we were about two-thirds of the way up, I noticed there was water to one side, the mountain's plumbing having come close to the stairs. Although there was nothing I could do with it, I reached for it, wanting to feel the control as I had everything else. The air could circulate, especially near the doors, so it didn't all feel marked. The earth couldn't go anywhere, but the water—that was different.

I could feel how pure it was as it flowed through the mountain and past the other elves. Reaching out farther, I followed the pipes with my mind as I walked.

I stopped when I felt the control of a familiar elf. Stepping toward the pipes, I tried to work out who it was and where.

It came to me after almost no time. It was Gwaelon, and he was trying to do something with the water.

"Ruehnar, I think I've found him," I said as loudly as I

dared. The water master came to my side, and I pointed in the direction I felt the control.

We paused, and I tried to show Ruehnar the location.

"I need to get to him. Do we have any earth elementals with us?" he asked.

There was only me, and I didn't hesitate to step toward the rock face.

Careful, Aella. We're going to need your strength for the coming fight, Zephyr pointed out.

I know, but we can't leave Gwaelon to die.

Remember what Ronan said.

I haven't forgotten, but we'd take this kind of risk for each other. It would be hypocritical and wrong if we didn't use a small amount of power to help our friends.

Zephyr didn't respond, but I felt the mix of emotions in him. He felt similarly, but he was also concerned that we were going to need everything I had.

As Ruehnar disappeared through the small hole I'd made him, tension crept through me. Who knew what other elves were out there and what they might do? I wanted to go after him and help, but I couldn't. The portal needed my attention, so I was going to have to keep going.

CHAPTER TWENTY-FIVE

When we reached the floor I was fairly sure the portal was on, I stopped. My legs ached from climbing so many sets of stairs, and I once again wished we'd been able to take the elevator. However, this would hopefully give us the element of surprise, and we were here in far greater numbers than the elevator would allow.

Stepping up to the wall, I reached out with my mind and made it thinner. It wasn't a quick process since the rock had to move gently so it didn't cause loud rumbles or shakes.

As soon as it got thin, I focused on one section at a time, making a hole the air elves could get through, then making it big enough for Zephyr. I saw the frustration on his face when everyone else was standing on the other side and I was still trying to enlarge it so he would fit.

I should take human form and help, Zephyr said, but I shook my head. Only a few of the elves here had seen him in human form, and I didn't plan on giving them that bit of information if I didn't have to.

We were going to keep going with him as a dragon, especially since I was hoping to be able to use his breath weapon.

As soon as we could all get through, I made my way back to Zephyr's side. Our eyes locked, and I knew he was considering taking human form to get through the gap. I shook my head imperceptibly, so concerned that I didn't think to use our telepathic link.

I don't want you to waste your power. Hiding your human form is worth it.

A deep rumble came out of his throat, but he waited while I widened the hole further. It took me longer than I wanted it to, and I was already fatigued.

Eat something, Zephyr reminded me.

Although I wanted to make a snarky comment about eating his tail or ask if he had pizza, I reached into one of my pockets and pulled out an energy bar.

At the same time, I waved the air elves on. They needed to find the portal and get the job done. I sent Sen and Roth with them since it would help me find them later.

This might not be a good idea, Zephyr said.

I know, but I don't have a better one. Cherisse is trying to get the portal open, and we can't have that. We have to throw everything at stopping them. And if that means we're putting ourselves more in danger, then that's what we've got to do.

That doesn't mean I have to like it.

I don't like it either.

We'd best hurry, then.

Well, it's not like anyone is helping.

You told me I couldn't, or I assure you I would be.

You're hot as a man, but I'd like to keep that to myself.

Zephyr chuckled before projecting the image of us from the previous night and how good he had looked without his top on.

It was a distracting mental image, but it made us feel less tense as I finally finished making the hole big enough for him. I went through first, reaching out with my mind to detect anyone coming toward us. Zephyr eased his way through the gap and shook, wiggling his wings.

Knowing roughly where the portal was, Sen and Roth moved toward it as I jogged. Zephyr easily kept up, his claws clicking on the stone floor.

I almost stopped in my tracks when Sen and the air elementals with her reached the portal area and Cherisse and the other elves came into view through Sen's mind. They were doing as I had feared. One standing near the portal held the tablet.

Zephyr picked up the pace as the air elves I'd brought with me hesitated. It did not surprise me that they weren't sure how to proceed. It was hard knowing how to fight other elves at the best of times. While they were risking their lives to break the pillars, the wrong attack could kill another elf.

By the time I reached the area, Cherisse had noticed the company. She wasn't near the barriers. The eight elves from the cult had formed a line there, backing up one who stood alone in the path of the fire, clutching the tablet they'd stolen.

I knew it was going to be difficult to stop this, but I couldn't hesitate like the others had. Taking control of the air, including inside the pillar-protected area, I blasted the cult elves backward with everything I had. I pushed them out of the force field, too far back to reach the pillars.

Several yelped in pain as I knocked them over, and it broke the awkward reluctance of the elves I'd brought up the mountain with me. As Cherisse whirled, having kept her balance and the other elves tried to scramble to their feet, the fight truly began.

Elements were hurled at us. Zephyr's scales blocked a ball of fire that came out of nowhere as I rocked the earth and took control of more of the air.

I kept moving forward, my eyes locked on Cherisse as she faced me, hurling water seemingly from nowhere. Roth got in the way, blocking and absorbing the water before turning it on another of her elves and sending him flying. Cherisse growled.

A moment later, an earth elf snatched control of the walls and floor. The stone shook beneath my feet, almost knocking me over, then tried to suck me under.

Several of the air elves around me suffered the same attack. I reached for control again, pushing back and trying to stop the assault before it pinned us all in place. It took a moment of wrestling back and forth as Roth and Zephyr continued to block water, fire, and air to help me stay safe.

I pushed harder, feeling my head begin to ache as I stretched my powers, but it worked and I was soon calming the rock beneath the feet of me and my allies again, allowing us to recover.

Cherisse took a different approach after that, pushing some of the elves with her back toward the pillars while the rest formed a barrier between us.

Given there were only eight of them, I'd expected to

overwhelm them with the group I had. However, they were powerful elves, and four throwing everything they could at us was enough to make it a difficult fight. I needed to find us an advantage and get things going in our favor.

There wasn't a lot I could do, however. My control of the elements was challenged at every turn, and some of the air elementals faced the same problem, depleting their powers. In here, the air was extremely marked since the cult was in their home, used to operating in the mountain.

A blast of water knocked another of my allies off his feet. I frowned and redoubled my efforts, but I was tiring.

Cherisse could sense it too, and her grin widened as she hurled more water. This time Roth didn't get there in time, and it hit me. I used the air around me to keep me from being knocked over, but I was distracted. A flood of water rushed over me, almost drowning me where I stood.

Zephyr rescued me, getting in the way of the blast and giving me a moment to recover. As the water flowed over him, I heard Cherisse yell something, but I couldn't see anything beyond the dragon and the water.

I reached for Sen's mind as Roth landed nearby and soaked up some of the water. The myconid was busy trying not to drown. An air elf lifted her out of the water and tucked her on a shoulder. She'd lost her little dart gun somewhere, and she was coughing and spluttering.

I hesitated. I'd been so focused on this battle that I'd lost sight of the mythicals I was bonded to and was supposed to be working with. Sen had been in trouble, and I'd not been there for her.

Focus, Aella, Zephyr's voice boomed. *We need your power.*

It was enough to snap me back to the present threat.

Without hesitation, I reached out and pulled at Cherisse's control of the water, forcing her back as I strode forward.

The water stopped hurtling toward Zephyr, and I could see again as I blasted her with more air. The elves were back in the portal area, trying to open the pillars. More of my air elves were down, one stuck under the water.

I ran to them, yanking them up as I took control of the rock around them to release them from their prisons. They spluttered as I held onto them. No one was dying today if I could help it.

I felt someone trying to win back control from me, and I could only hold my ground for a moment.

We need to stop them from opening the portal, Zephyr said. He roared and took a few steps forward before being hit with more fire.

I put it out with water, creating a concentrated stream, and then I turned my attention to the portal and the elf in the field. It was the young fire elf that must have recently come into her powers.

But there were still too many elves in my way. I couldn't get to her to stop her, and I didn't dare stop the elves supporting her or I'd kill her.

We need more help, I said to Zephyr, fear rising in my chest. *I can't get to the elf in the field.*

Before he could respond, I heard someone splashing up the tunnel. I turned to see Gwaelon and Ruehnar rushing up. As they did, they took control of the water around them, seeming to know they were needed.

I smiled as they blasted Cherisse with it, knocking her off her feet and staggering the elf next to her. It gave me the confidence I needed to reach for the air in the portal field. I noticed that the field didn't feel right. The girl was dominating the pillar, and it was no longer fighting her as hard.

I could see the tablet in her hands glowing, absorbing the power of the pillars or something like that. My mind was able to feel the transfer, but I could not figure it out.

"Stop her," Zephyr said. "Before it's too late."

Not sure what else to do, I hurled all the air I could at the group of elves and fought for control of the air in the pillar area, but she held her ground, and I knew it wouldn't be long now.

I pulled out the dart gun I carried and shot without hesitation. The first dart missed, blasted off-track before I could stop it. When I tried again, it hit one of the elves helping the woman. I moved forward when I saw the girl screw up her face in pain.

"Get out of there," I yelled as the elf I'd hit passed out.

The girl only glanced my way, focused as she was on the pillar. I did the only thing I could think of; I took control of the earth in the pillar, snatching it from her. It was as if her mind broke. She screamed and slumped, her body smoking and writhing.

As she kneeled, she let go of the tablet. It fell, shattering into thousands of pieces and losing any power it had.

I tried to take control of the air again and pull her out with it, but I was met by resistance as the pillar recovered from the assault on it and reclaimed the area.

My mind was shoved out before I could gather my strength and try again.

I felt Gwaelon's hand on my shoulder as I continued to try to think of a way to get her out.

"It's too late," the water elf said aloud. "She chose this fate. She knew the risks. You can't save her."

Not sure I could stop, I tried anyway, heading closer and fighting for control of the air. I was aware of the battle around me and one of the elves in the cult screaming things at me, but I didn't care. I continued to fight forward, blasting friend and foe alike back from the portal area to reach the girl.

I pulled her smoking, burned, distorted body out of the forcefield. I had to reach in, and my arm burned as I did.

By the time I got her out and sank to my knees beside her, Zephyr was by my side, his tail sweeping up and around me. I leaned into him as I cried.

I'd killed this young elf.

There was no way she was as old as me, and she'd just been beginning her journey as a fire elemental.

Gwaelon was right, Zephyr said. *There was nothing you could have done. But we've done what we needed, and we have to leave now.*

I blinked, the words Zephyr had projected bringing back the situation and what we needed to do.

I'd stopped the elves here. One elf they needed was dead, and the tablet was broken. They couldn't open their portal anymore.

Sen bounded toward me, her mushroom top dripping water, and I reached for her and tucked her into my jacket.

It was time to go.

Zephyr stayed on one side of me as we moved away from the portal. The cult elves had withdrawn to a small pocket with Cherisse, and Gwaelon was holding them there with a wall of water.

"It's done. We can go," I said. "Let the water down, and all of you get back down the stairs as swiftly as you can."

Gwaelon looked as if he might argue, but he nodded and backed up.

As soon as the wall of water fell, I stepped forward. My eyes fixed on the face of a male elf near the back before he turned, jostled by the elves around him who were trying to get to me. I could have sworn I knew him, but not where from.

"I didn't want anyone to die, but the portals can't be opened," I said as Cherisse tried to attack, the moment pushing all thoughts of the strange yet familiar face out of my head. I didn't have time to work out where I'd seen him, not when this situation was still precarious and I needed and wanted to leave.

I took control of all the earth, water, and air around us and made sure the few elves before me couldn't. I felt several of them trying, but they were exhausted, and I had the upper hand. They soon gave up and simply stood before me, the fight gone from all of them, including Cherisse.

"I'm sorry," I said a moment later, the pain on their faces registering. "I know this means a lot to you, but evil lingers on the other side of those portals. I can't let you plunge this entire planet into a war it will lose even if we beat whoever is behind it."

Without another word, I strode off, following Zephyr as we made our way back down the mountain. We didn't meet anyone, and the flashlights still lit the way. Despite knowing we were all safe, I felt wrong, my body and mind numb. All I could think about was the young dead elf, still clutching a shattered tablet.

When we got to the bottom of the mountain, I expected to have to fight my way out, but the allied forces had gotten the better of the elves. We all rushed outside, blinking in the bright light.

"Mission accomplished?" the major asked when he saw me.

I couldn't reply; my voice was stuck in my throat. How did I tell them all I'd killed the biggest threat? That there was the life of someone deluded but still valuable on my hands.

"We've done what was needed," Zephyr replied for me a moment later.

Minsheng came up and wrapped his arms around me. Gwaelon stood behind him. The water elemental must have told my Shishou what had happened.

Without warning, the tears fell, and I sobbed into his shoulder.

EPILOGUE

I tried not to think about anything but the beauty of the moment, flying on Zephyr as we made our way north. Roth and Sen were coasting in our slipstream as we traveled.

After everything that had happened, we'd taken several days to get away from our lives and relax together. And to travel.

In my bag was the envelope my adoptive parents had given me, and we were using it to guide us now. The Canadian border was behind us, and we were flying over the forests and rivers that stretched below.

It wouldn't be much longer until the town came into sight. We'd used a satnav to direct us for the last part of the journey, although it seemed confused because we could fly over any obstacle or building to get where we wanted to go.

Most important, we were only a few miles out and able to come down lower. I wanted to scope out the area and get an idea if this was a mythical trying to hide and if we would draw attention he didn't want to him.

I wanted answers, and I had a feeling that this guy had a few. Shuddering, I thought back to the brief moment inside the cult mountain. The face I'd briefly seen had looked a lot like the man in my photo. It had been a glance, however, and I couldn't be sure.

Still can't shake the idea that it was him? Zephyr asked as he swung lower, the smudge on the horizon growing into a town with distinct houses.

No. I mean, I don't know for certain whether it was or wasn't him, but it looked a lot like him.

And you want to ask this guy questions? Not get backup?

It's one person.

You're one person.

Good point, I replied, but I wasn't worried. I might only be one person, but I was backed up by three amazing mythicals. It wasn't hard for them to buy me time to harness my powers.

I sighed as I thought back to that moment at the mountain in Mexico, and it brought back the pain of killing another elf. I'd killed people before, but there was something about the way this had happened. I'd never directly taken the life of another mythical, even in battle. It had always been about exhausting the other's magic.

Every time I closed my eyes, I saw the mangled elven body I'd pulled out of the pillar's field of control. It had been my fault; no matter what anyone told me, I knew I'd been the person to end her life.

Of course, I also knew I wished not to have needed to.

I'd been in a situation where I had to act, and now I had to live with the consequences.

I heard a small growl from Zephyr and felt a wave of affection from him. I felt better. I wasn't alone. He was there to help me through it.

Pushing the upsetting thoughts out of my head, I focused on the town and how many people were about. It was late in the afternoon, the town growing colder as the sun threatened to set on us.

Before long, we'd scoped the town out and concluded that it was quiet, with few people out at this time. We were probably safe to land as long as we were discreet.

With that in mind, I opted to go down alone and land in the backyard of the house we had traced to this guy. It made my stomach churn since I hoped I'd find him there, looking different from his photo. I hadn't seen him in the mountain helping Cherisse and the rest of her crazy cult.

I walked slowly to the screen door at the back of the house to see if there was movement beyond and someone was there. There were no signs of occupation, so I pulled it open and stepped inside. It took a moment for my eyes to adjust before I noticed that the interior was messy.

The kitchen was covered in pots and pans full of the residue of an easily reheatable meal. The table was covered in discarded plates. A small desk sat in the corner. It had no computer on it, only a bunch of papers and notes.

Although the back of the building smelled awful, I went over to the notes, puzzled. Where was this guy's computer? For that matter, where was he?

"Hello?" I called.

There was nothing but silence as I tried to work out what to do next.

A moment later, Zephyr and the rest of my mythicals descended. There was no point in them hiding so we didn't freak this guy out if he wasn't here.

I moved deeper into the house, exploring, but all I found was the appearance of a struggle. The furniture in the sitting room had been knocked around, and there was a shattered vase on the floor with a single flower in.

There wasn't anything else to go on—no sign of my quarry, and no way to know where he'd gone.

Zephyr landed, and I asked him what he made of it.

Something spooked him before we got here. Check his notes.

Not disagreeing, I checked notes covering the desk, seeing formulas and all sorts of other things. It was gibberish to me until I found a few that talked about a cache of something written in Elvish. Several pieces of information had been circled, and they seemed to indicate that this guy had found a collection of stone tablets. There were pictures of archaeological digs full of them.

As I thought of the havoc a single tablet had wreaked and how we'd almost seen the portal open, fear rippled through me. There were more of them. Lots more. I couldn't let them fall into the wrong hands.

We'll find them first, Zephyr said. *Whatever it takes.*

Whatever it takes.

The story continues with *Pegasus Souled*, book 9 in the Dragon of Shadow and Air series.

Claim your copy today!

ACKNOWLEDGMENTS

It seems only right to begin by thanking my publisher LMBPN and everyone in it. There are so many people in the company who handle my books at various stages and do an amazing job of getting it ready for publication after I finish the general drafting. I am still blown away by how lovely everyone is and how many people give me their time and expertise and always with a smile. You're beginning to feel like family. The place my books have always belonged.

And a big thank you to Bear and David yet again for helping with the plot. This book was probably one of the hardest to figure out so far and I didn't have a clear idea of it at first. But we got there in the end and your collective insight was invaluable.

To Bryan. For understanding so much on so many levels. For encouraging me at every turn. And for making me feel as if I could maybe achieve some semblance of greatness even when all the world around me wants to try and tell me I don't mean anything to anyone.

And finally to God. For having a plan and being there in the small moments and the big and letting me know that I'm somehow always enough.

ABOUT THE AUTHOR

Jess was born in the quaint village of Woodbridge in the UK, has spent some of her childhood in the States and now resides near the beautiful Roman city of Bath. She lives with her husband, Phil, her two tiny humans (one boy and one girl) and her very dapsy cat, Pleaides.

During her still relatively short life Jess has displayed an innate curiosity for learning new things and has therefore studied many subjects, from maths and the sciences, to history and drama. Jess now works full time as a writer and mummy, incorporating many of the subjects she has an interest in within her plots and characters.

When she's not busy with work and keeping her tiny humans alive she can often be found with friends, playing with miniature characters, dice and pieces of paper covered in funny stats and notes about fictional adventures her figures have been on.

You can find out more about the author and her upcoming projects by joining her on facebook, by watching her live D&D_streams,_or emailing her via books@jessmountifield.co.uk. Jess loves hearing from a happy fan so please do get in touch!

Jess is also opening up her discord for fans to come chat about what she's up to, and see a few sneak peaks of future work. There's also a chance to become one of her beta readers. If you'd like to check that out you can do so here.

Connect with Jess Mountifield

Mailing list sign up
Facebook group.
Discord group
Actual play D&D stream: Twitch or Youtube
Email address: contact me here.

Already published

Urban Fantasy

Dragon of Shadow and Air:

Air Bound (Book 1)

Shadow Sworn (Book 2)

Dragon Souled (Book 3)

Earth Bound (Book 4)

Night Sworn (Book 5)

Dryad Souled (Book 6)

Water Bound (Book 7)

Day Sworn (Book 8)

Pegasus Souled (Book 9)

Fantasy

Tales of Ethanar:

Wandering to Belong (Tale 1)

Innocent Hearts (Tale 2 & 3)

For Such a Time as This (Tale 4)

A Fire's Sacrifice (Tale 5)

Winter Series:

The Hope of Winter (Tale 6.05)

The Fire of Winter (Tale 6.1)

Guild of the Eternal Flame:

Wayfarer's Sanctuary

Protector's Secret

Healer's Oath

Other Fantasy:

The Initiate (under Holly Lujah)

Writing with Dawn Chapman:

Jessica's Challenge (#5 in the Puatera Online series)

Dahlia's Shadow (#6 in the Puatera Online series)

Lila's Revenge (#7 in the Puatera Online series)

Sci-Fi:

Fringe Colonies:

Alliance

Haven

Rebellion

Rebirth

Reclamation

Star Trail:

Hunted

Sherdan series:

Sherdan's Prophecy

Sherdan's Legacy

Sherdan's Country

Sherdan's Road (A short story in the anthology 'The End of the Road')

The Slave Who'd Never Been Kissed (A short in the charity anthology 'Imaginings')

New Beginnings

Santa's Little Space Pirate

In the multi-author Adamanta series:

Episode 1 – Adamanta

Episode 3 – Excelsior

Episode 8 – Phoenix

Episode 13 – New Contacts

Episode 17 – Sacrifice

Other:

Clues, Claws and Christmas

Non-Fic:

How to Write Lots, and Get Sh*t Done: the Art of Not Being a Flake

Find purchase links here

Coming soon:

Urban Fantasy:

Dragon of Shadow and Air:

Fire Bound

Light Sworn

Phoenix Souled

Fantasy

(Tales of Ethanar):

The Pursuit of Winter (#2 in the Winter series, Tale 6.2)

Books under Amelia Price

Mycroft Holmes Adventures:

The Hundred Year Wait

The Unexpected Coincidence

The Invisible Amateur

The Female Charm

The Reluctant Knight

The Ambitious Orphan

The Unconventional Honeymoon Gift

The Family Reunion

The Immortal Problem

Coming soon:

The Unremarkable Assistant